"His latest extravaganza of comic pizzazz"

—*The Washington Post Book World*

"For imaginative plot and decorative detail, Mr. Pinkwater's scores go off the charts."

—*The New York Times*

"Combining wisdom and wackiness in equal measure, Pinkwater's cool style blows over a series of searing inventions; he is a writer to love."

—Samuel R. Delany

"I admire Mr. Pinkwater for his outrageous silliness, for his sympathy for avocados and other strange beings, and for his occasional lapses into serious and delicate fantasy."

—Vonda N. McIntyre

Pinkwater is often hilarious . . . a riotous revelation."

—*Kliatt*

"Comic, bizarre and brilliantly written"

—Stuart, FL *News*

DANIEL M. PINKWATER

Young ADULTS

TOR

A TOM DOHERTY ASSOCIATES BOOK
NEW YORK

YOUNG ADULTS

Copyright © 1985 by Daniel M. Pinkwater
Young Adult Novel (c) 1982 by Daniel Pinkwater

A Tor Book
Published by Tom Doherty Associates, Inc.
49 West 24th Street
New York, N.Y. 10010

ISBN: 0-812-51519-6

Printed in the United States of America

First edition: November 1985
First mass market printing: August 1991

Printed in the United States of America

0 9 8 7 6 5 4 3 2 1

Contents

Young Adult Novel

1

Kevin's new social worker was Mr. Justin Jarvis, and Kevin didn't like him one bit. He was constantly smiling, and he spoke in a smooth, soft voice that made Kevin nervous.

Most annoying was the knowledge that Kevin depended on Mr. Jarvis completely. Kevin's mother was in the madhouse. Mr. Jarvis called it a psychiatric facility—but it was a madhouse, nothing else—and Kevin's mother was mad. She had gone mad the day Kevin's father had been in the accident at the methane works—the day he had been deprived of speech, sight, and hearing, and the use of his legs. Dad was in the veteran's hospital now, little better than a vegetable. When Kevin was taken to visit his father, all he could do was sit and stare at the broken form in the wheelchair. His father horrified him, and made him feel angry. How could you leave me like this? Kevin thought.

What was Scott Shapiro, Kevin's father, thinking about in the wheelchair? Was he remembering the day he had been blown into darkness and silence forever by the exploding methane tank? Was he remembering that last morning, before the accident, before his wife, Cynthia, had gone mad? Was he remembering the news that had come that morning, that Kevin's sister, Isobel, had been arrested for prostitution?

As far as Kevin knew, Isobel was still downtown, working the bars across the street from the bus station. He wished he could talk to her. Isobel had always been the only one in the Shapiro family who understood Kevin.

Maybe some day Isobel would be brought in to the alcoholism treatment center where Kevin was staying. There was always a chance of that. Kevin had done his earliest drinking with Isobel.

If the vice squad ever caught her, they might bring her to the alcoholism treatment center. She wouldn't be sent to regular jail—after all, she was only fifteen—just two years older than Kevin.

Kevin felt the wad of money in his sock. He had earned sixty-five dollars that morning, selling pills to the other kids in the treatment center. In addition, he had twenty dollars he had stolen from Mr. Jarvis.

So here was Kevin, a thirteen-year-old alcoholic, pusher, and thief. His mother would probably never get well, his father certainly wouldn't, and his sister, Isobel, was turning tricks on State Street. It seemed to Kevin that there wasn't a chance in the world that he would ever get his life straightened out.

And he was right. So we hit him over the head and fed him to the pigs.

2

This is Charles the Cat speaking. The sad story of Kevin, the messed-up thirteen-year-old, is one of the pastimes of the Wild Dada Ducks. It is a story entitled *Kevin Shapiro, Boy Orphan*. The Wild Dada Ducks tell this story to one another. Each Wild Dada Duck makes up as much of the story as he likes, and the story is always changing. Sometimes Kevin is an orphan, sometimes a juvenile delinquent, a druggie, a lonely child of feuding parents, a social misfit, a homosexual, a weakling who wants to play sports, and any number of other kinds of hard-luck characters.

Kevin Shapiro, Boy Orphan is different from

7

the novels in the Himmler High School library in that he never solves his problems. Instead, we usually kill him from time to time. Kevin is indestructible. You can kill him as often as you like. He can be brought back to life in the next chapter, which usually gets told the following day during lunch.

In addition to myself, Charles the Cat, the other Wild Dada Ducks are the Honorable Venustiano Carranza (President of Mexico), Captain Colossal, Igor, and the Indiana Zephyr. Those are not our real names—they are our Dada names. We don't use our real names anymore.

There is also the Duckettes, the Wild Dada Ducks ladies' auxiliary, which has no member at all at present. Should suitable females present themselves for membership in the Duckettes, we will consider them, but there have been no applicants as yet. Dada is generally a misunderstood art movement.

It was the Honorable Venustiano Carranza (President of Mexico) who first told us about Dada. In those days El Presidente was known as Pecos Bill. When we heard about Dada, we all agreed to devote our lives to it, took new names, and began our historically important work of reshaping culture, righting the wrongs of the past, and producing new works of Dada Art. Starting with Himmler High School, we intend to bring about a world Dada Renaissance. We have already written a Wild Dada Duck Manifesto.

The Wild Dada Duck Manifesto

On this, the natal day of Marcel Duchamp
(the first Tuesday of every month at 4:00 P.M.),
the Board of Medical Advisors of the Empire
of Japan declares that the institution
formerly known as Margaret Himmler High
School will henceforth become the Municipal
Vacuum Cleaner. Teachers will report for
reprocessing as diesel railroad locomotives,
and students will adopt the appearance and
function of electrocomputerized kitchen
appliances. Those who choose not to comply
with the ruling of the Imperial Medical Board
will be required to present a paper cup not
filled with cherry pits or gravel at the office
of the ex-administrator of unexpected nasal
events. All others will be required to present
paper cups *not* filled with cherry pits or
gravel at the nose of the official administrator
of ex-events. By this simple measure, world
peace, brotherhood and unlimited happiness
has been secured for all mechanohumanoids.

Fellow machines! Dis-unite! This call to
arms, torsos, and feet will not be repeated
except by request.

One hundred thousand copies of the Wild
Dada Duck Manifesto, printed on black paper
with black ink were not made, and were not distributed to the students and faculty of Himmer
High. This was the first important action of the

Daniel M. Pinkwater

Wild Dada Ducks, and it was met, as we hoped it would be, with wild indifference.

By the way, it turns out that the Honorable Venustiano Carranza (President of Mexico) had not made Dada up in his own head. It is a real movement, and Marcel Duchamp was a real person. I found that out only after being a Dadaist myself for months.

3

At this point I would like to describe the members of the Wild Dada Ducks. The Honorable Venustiano Carranza (President of Mexico) is tall and thin. The Indiana Zephyr is tall and thin. I, Charles the Cat, am not tall, and thin. Captain Colossal is tall and not thin. Igor is not tall and not thin. Because Dada is a serious movement, we try to remain dignified in expression and dress. We laugh as little as possible, at least in the presence of others, and we always wear neckties. My favorite necktie is black with red plastic fish about five inches long attached to it with miracle glue. The Honorable Venustiano Carranza (President of Mexico) has a wheel from a baby carriage which he wears on a chain around his neck, over his tie. Igor has a banana on a string which he wears around his neck. He talks with the banana, whose name is Freddie, and also uses it as a mock microphone and make-believe pistol. Captain Colossal and the Indiana Zephyr are also stylish, but they do not have one favorite kind of attire—they alter their appearance from day to day.

This brings me to the response to the presence of the Wild Dada Ducks on the part of the other students at Himmler High. I am sorry to say that a great many of them are hostile to our Dadaistic expression of our innermost feelings. I am even sorrier to say that many more of the Himmler students are not hostile. They are totally indifferent. As far as I know, the Wild Dada Ducks have no active supporters in the school—not even any sympathizers. In a nutshell, they don't care about us, or they hate us. This includes teachers.

Of course, being resourceful Dadaists, we have decided to capitalize on the situation as it exists. Our every move as Wild Dada Ducks is calculated to make people ignore or detest us all the more. In this way, the population of Himmler High is doing what we want it to without knowing it.

Of course we don't take any of the indifference or abuse personally. It is not as individuals that we are hated and ignored, but as Dadaists. What is more, we recognize our responsibility to educate and enlighten the people at Himmler.

And so, we are very busy Wild Dada Ducks. Some examples: In the main hall of Himmler High there is a large glass display case. It has electric lights in it, and was formerly used to display trophies won by the school's teams. Some time ago vandals opened the case and stole the trophies. There was a big uproar about it. As Wild Dada Ducks, we approved of this—feeling that the vandals might be groping their way toward Dadaism—and wrote a letter to the school paper saying so. The letter was never printed. The Wild Dada Ducks discussed this, and decided that the school was unable to deal with our clear-sighted philosophical analysis of the theft because it was grieving over the loss of the trophies. As a humanitarian gesture, we decided to give the school a new trophy, a better one than all the ones that had been stolen.

It was easily done. First we went to a junkyard and bought a fine used toilet—just the bowl, without the tank or seat. This we lovingly cleaned and polished until it was very beautiful, and looked much better than new. The only difficult part was getting access to the empty display case—but since there was nothing in it, it wasn't particularly closely watched. With a giant pair of pliers Igor smashed the dinky cheap lock on the case. We then placed the shining, lovely toilet in the case. (We had smuggled the art object, wrapped in brown paper, into the school the day before.) We turned on the electric lights. Then we replaced the dinky cheap lock with a new, beautiful one, made of brass, and very shiny. To prevent future vandals from getting into the case, we left the keys for the lock inside, next to the beautiful toilet. We had polished them too.

The total effect was wonderful! The toilet bowl gleamed in the warm electric light, and made all the Wild Dada Ducks very proud and happy. Now all the people at Himmler would be able to take pride again. Now there was a trophy even finer and more significant in place of the cheap ordinary ones that had been stolen. What was more, now all the people at Himmler would have a chance to think about what a beautiful object a toilet is! We had done a heroic thing.

And was it appreciated? Of course not! There were only two opinions expressed by all who saw our work of art. Some thought it was terrible, and some thought it was funny. However, everybody came to see it, and nothing else was talked about for the two days the toilet remained in the case, shining like a beacon of truth in the main hall of Himmler High.

The principal had our magnificently polished lock removed with a hacksaw, and the art work was removed and discarded—it would wind up on the same dump we had gotten it from.

Everybody suspected that we were the artists, but we remained silent. After all, we did not do what we did for credit, but for the benefit of mankind.

And now a word about Dada music. The Wild Dada Ducks are happy to note that there's a lot of very acceptable Dada music being performed these days. This is the only area in which the kids at Himmler show any signs of culture. Some of the groups approved by the Wild Dada Ducks are the Slugs, the Yeggs, the Noggs, and the Yobs.

4

Kevin Shapiro, Boy Orphan, Chapter One Thousand Fifteen:

Kevin didn't want anyone to see him thinking about Aunt Lucille, because whenever he thought about her there was a good chance he might cry. It made Kevin feel all soft and weepy when he remembered sitting in front of the huge stone fireplace at Red Oaks, Aunt Lucille's great house in the Kentucky bluegrass country. There, Kevin had had his own little room up in the attic, and his own Thoroughbred horse to train and ride. Winky was the name of Kevin's horse, and he had fed him and cared for him from the time he was a little colt. It had looked as though Winky had a great future as a racer, and Kevin was going to ride him in the Kentucky Derby.

All that changed the day Kevin was sent to Lexington with Simms, the handyman. They had driven over in Aunt Lucille's Rolls-Royce to get a new silver snaffle for Winky. How could Kevin have known that something would go horribly wrong at the nuclear reactor in Cogginsville, just two miles away from Red Oaks? How could Kevin have known that Aunt Lucille and Winky, and all the other horses, and Red Oaks itself would light up with a strange blue glow, and that the entire place would be put off limits, and quarantined forever by the Atomic Energy Commission? Kevin would never see Winky and Aunt Lucille again—and how was he to know? Still, Kevin felt that somehow it was all his fault.

Another artistic project of the Wild Dada Ducks was our play, *Chickens from Uranus*, a science-fiction thriller. We made wonderful posters to announce our play. They had pictures of heavy machinery and really nice angular lettering that Igor does. It's almost illegible.

We put the play on in the lunchroom. Here it is:

Chickens from Uranus
Adapted from *Macbeth*
by William Shakespeare

Dramatis Personae

Tick and Tock, *two Roman emperors*
Lord Buddha, *a rock star*
Henry Ford, *a teenage starlet*
The Devil, *the devil*
(All the characters appear wearing paper bags over their heads. The bags are decorated with cutouts of pictures of bulldozers, tractors, military tanks, automobiles, and chickens.)

TICK: Moo! Moo! Moo! Moo!
TOCK: Arf! Arf! Arf! Arf!
BUDDHA: Woo! Woo! Woo! Woo!
H. FORD: Meow! Meow! Meow! Meow!
THE DEVIL: *(Whistles like a bird)*
ALL: *(Leafing through a deck of cards)* Three of clubs. Jack of diamonds. Two of clubs. Ace of diamonds. Five of hearts. Queen of spades. Two of spades. King of clubs . . . *(and so on until all the cards have been read).*
ALL: *(Hum)* Mmmmmmmmmmmm.
Mmmmmmmmmmm.
Mmmmmmmmmmm.

Finis

It isn't much of a script in terms of length, but the actual performance took a good twenty minutes because we spoke extremely slowly, and moved very slowly, like robots. It was a great performance, and to prove it, nobody paid any attention to it. The best actor was Captain Colossal, who had the part of Henry Ford. It took him almost half a minute just to say "meow."

Amazingly, we were summoned by the Lord High Executioner (that's Mr. Gerstenblut, the vice-principal), as a result of our performance. He said that Himmler High School did not approve of our activities. He said that we had disrupted the lunch period by putting on an unauthorized play. Naturally, we thanked him for praising us, at which point he got angry. He shouted at us. He also told us that we were in violation of the Himmler High School Dress Code by wearing fish and baby-carriage wheels around our necks. And lobsters. On this particular day the Indiana Zephyr was wearing a very large red plastic lobster which we all admired.

Mr. Gerstenblut told us that if we didn't shape up we'd be in trouble.

Even though the Wild Dada Ducks are pacific, peaceful, nonviolent, and even ultra-nonviolent, we will not run from a fight if there is no other way. It was clear to us that Mr. Gerstenblut was making an ultimatum which could lead to only one response. War.

Kevin Shapiro, Boy Orphan, Chapter Six Thousand Four Hundred and One.

Kevin's head was swimming. Could it be? Was it possible, after only doing it once? Of course, he'd heard of it happening to other kids, but somehow he had never considered it as something that could happen to him. After all, Brenda knew what she was doing—she had told him so. She had said not to worry. Kevin had believed her. He had trusted her. He knew Brenda wouldn't lie, but now, here he was, looking at the doctor's face, which loomed as large as a face on a movie screen. The doctor had a kindly expression, but it all seemed like some kind of horrible nightmare. "Yes, there's no doubt about it," the doctor was saying to Kevin, "you are two months pregnant."

5

The most aggravating thing the Lord High Executioner said to us was that since the Wild Dada Ducks was not an officially sanctioned Himmler High School student activity, as far as he was concerned, the Wild Dada Ducks did not exist.

We held a council of war. It was decided that we could not overlook this insult. Venustiano Carranza (President of Mexico) made a stirring speech. Igor and the Indiana Zephyr wanted to engage in prolonged terrorism, but Captain Colossal reminded them that any action we might take should be in keeping with our Dadaist principles.

There was some discussion of flooding the library and holding war canoe races there as a gesture of indifference to Mr. Gerstenblut's ill-mannered remark. While everyone agreed that the idea had merit, and it would be worth looking into for some future activity, it was generally felt that our response to Mr. Gerstenblut's insolence should be expressed more directly, even though that would not be the most Dada approach.

Finally, it was decided that since the Lord High Executioner had questioned our existence, the appropriate response would be to bring his existence into question.

It was agreed that we would issue a public statement of Mr. Gerstenblut's lack of reality, failure to be, and nonpresence in the world as we know it.

Captain Colossal printed up several hundred cards in the print shop. To make it classier, we printed them in French.

Horace Gerstenblut
n'existe pas.

Since less than three percent of the kids at Himmler take French, there was considerable interest in the cards. People didn't know what they said. Also, we distributed them in an interesting way. We put stacks of them in the bathrooms of both sexes. People picked them up when they went to the bathroom, and handed them around.

Not only did we have revenge on Mr. Gertenblut, it was also the most successful work of Art so far undertaken by the Wild Dada Ducks. That is, it was the first thing we had done in which people had taken such an active interest. We were a little sorry we hadn't printed something about Dada on the card.

We knew the cards were a big success because Igor takes French, and dozens of people asked him to translate the *Horace Gerstenblut n'existe pas* cards they were carrying around with them.

We didn't know how much of a success the cards were until the last period of the day, during which we were called out of our respective classes and assembled in the office of the Lord High Executioner.

Mr. Gerstenblut had fifteen or twenty cards on his desk. "What do you fellows know about this?" he asked, handing the cards to each of us.

"It's in French," Captain Colossal said.

"It has your name on it," I said.

"It says that you don't exist," Igor said.

25

"And what do you weirdos have to do with these?" Mr. Gerstenblut asked.

"I'm afraid we can't tell you," Venustiano Carranza (President of Mexico) said.

"And why not?"

"Because you don't exist."

Kevin Shapiro, Boy Orphan, Chapter Eleven Thousand Six Hundred.

So that was why it had been the easiest fight Kevin had ever been in. No wonder the new kid hadn't been able to land a single punch. "That's right, you miserable skunk," Mr. Jarvis said, "you beat up a blind boy." Kevin felt the hot tears well up in his eyes—his eyes that could see. Mr. Jarvis was right—he was a miserable skunk. How could he have been so stupid? What made it worse, Kevin sort of liked the new kid. He hadn't wanted to fight him. Something had caused Kevin to lose all control when the kid made that remark about homosexuals. Kevin wondered what had made him so mad. And he really liked the kid.

Mr. Gerstenblut told us that he was going to let us off because he didn't have any proof—but he was going to watch us. He said that we were nihilists, and he wasn't going to stand for any of that at Himmler.

We looked up *nihilist* in the library. We were tickled. Of course we weren't nihilists—

Dadaists are constructive artists—but we all agreed, if we couldn't have been Dadaists, nihilists would have been a fairly decent second choice.

6

Imagine our surprise when we found out that there was a kid actually named Kevin Shapiro in the school! The Indiana Zephyr was the one to first discover this item of historically important information. The Wild Dada Ducks were all excited to think that there was an actual person bearing the name of the hero of our communal creation, *Kevin Shapiro, Boy Orphan.*

"Who is this kid?" Igor asked. "What does he look like?"

"We will adopt him," the Honorable Venustiano Carranza (President of Mexico) said. "Kevin Shapiro will be an orphan no more!"

"Yes," I said, "we should adopt this flesh-and-

29

Daniel M. Pinkwater

blood Kevin Shapiro in honor of the hero of our Dada young-adult novel."

"But let's keep our interest in the fortunate young man a secret!" the Indiana Zephyr said.

"A dark secret," said Igor.

"Good! Good!" said the Honorable Venustiano Carranza (President of Mexico). "We will become the secret helpers of this Kevin Shapiro."

"We will help him to lead a full, rich, Dadaistic life!" I shouted.

"And he will never know who is helping him!" Captain Colossal said.

We were all getting very excited about the existence of a real-life Kevin Shapiro.

To tell the truth, we had all been getting fairly fed up with the Kevin Shapiro story we took turns telling, and I, for one, had the feeling that it might be time to kill him off once and for all. Now, the news that there was a real Kevin, and that he was going to be unknowingly adopted by the Wild Dada Ducks, breathed new life into our little artistic circle.

The only Wild Dada Duck who knew what the real Kevin Shapiro looked like was the Indiana Zephyr. We got up from the table where we had been discussing this remarkable development and went for a little stroll around the lunchroom, so the Indiana Zephyr could point out our new adoptee.

It never fails to strike me, when the Wild Dada Ducks go anywhere, what a dignified and

30

impressive picture we must make. Dressed in the finest Dada taste, serious, and intelligent looking, the Wild Dada Ducks are as fine a body of young men as anyone could hope to see.

We made our little promenade around the lunchroom, the Indiana Zephyr looking for our darling child, Kevin Shapiro. At last he pointed him out. "That's him over there," the Indiana Zephyr whispered.

Kevin Shapiro was better than any of us could have hoped. He was perfect. In fact, he was wonderful. He was magnificent. He was short, maybe five two, and skinny. His hair was pale blond, and he wore it in a style known as a flattop. This is a crew cut with the hair standing up straight. The hair at the sides of the head is longer than the hair at the top of the head. The total effect is that of making one's head appear flat. It's a 1950s style that has come back into fashion because of some pre-Dada rock groups. Kevin Shapiro also had glasses, big cumbersome-looking plastic ones. His skin was very pale, and he had a little nose. We fell in love with him instantly.

Kevin Shapiro, never dreaming of his good fortune, was hunched over a box of Grape-Nuts, which he had opened by pulling apart the flaps on the side of the box, along the dotted lines. Into the waxed paper lining of the box Kevin Shapiro had poured the contents of a carton of milk. The milk was dribbling out the corners of the box as he ate the cereal with a plastic spoon.

"This is auspicious," the Honorable Venustiano Carranza (President of Mexico) said to the rest of the Wild Dada Ducks. "Grape-Nuts is a Dada food, especially when you eat it out of the carton like that."

"Munch on, little Kevin Shapiro," Captain Colossal said under his breath. "The Wild Dada Ducks will watch over you from this day forward."

7

"The first thing we ought to do," said the Honorable Venustiano Carranza (President of Mexico), "before we start helping Kevin Shapiro, is to find out all we can about the adorable little fellow."

This is the reason that the Honorable Venustiano Carranza (President of Mexico) is the undisputed leader of the Wild Dada Ducks. His foresight and methodical thinking is equalled only by his great artistic talent and Dadaistic style. It was agreed then and there, in the lunchroom, while Kevin Shapiro was finishing up his Grape-Nuts, that we would do exhaustive research about our little adopted boy.

Each of us, without being obvious or calling attention to himself, would endeavor to find out all there was to find out about Kevin. In this way, the Honorable Venustiano Carranza (President of Mexico) pointed out, we would be able to see if there were any areas of deficiency in the life of our little adoptling. We would begin by supplying whatever Kevin lacked. Later we would help him to become a great culture hero—all without ever revealing ourselves, of course.

It was agreed that the following day, after school, we would meet at the Balkan Falcon Drug Company across the street from Himmler High and discuss the information we had gathered.

The Balkan Falcon Drug Company is our favorite meeting place. It is generally shunned by other Himmler High students because of the foul temper of the fat old lady behind the counter, and the poor quality of the soda fountain—warm soda, filthy spoons, inedible hamburgers, and the like. However, the Wild Dada Ducks like the place because it has booths, it's never crowded, and raisin toast costs only twenty cents an order.

So it was that the Wild Dada Ducks gathered at the Balkan Falcon Drug Company after school the following afternoon. Having been insulted by the fat old lady behind the counter, and having provided ourselves with raisin toast and hot chocolate in grimy cups, we proceeded to report to one another on what we had learned about our dear little Kevin Shapiro.

As each Wild Dada Duck spoke, I took notes. When everyone had made his report, I read back to the others all I had written:

Kevin Shapiro is a freshman. He is an average student, and likes biology best of all his classes. His least favorite class is physical education, in which class his performance is perfectly miserable. He is nearsighted, and wears his glasses all the time. He lives in an apartment in one of the new buildings near Mesmer Park with his parents. He has no brothers or sisters. Kevin's family has a late-model Japanese sedan, a color television, and an old cocker spaniel named Henry, who is overweight. Kevin walks Henry twice a day—before he leaves for school, and when he returns in the afternoon. In the evening Kevin's father walks Henry. Kevin has few friends. Those people he does know are mostly involved in comic-book collecting. None of them go to Himmler. Kevin has a fairly large collection of old comic books, and almost every Saturday he goes around the city, looking for comics in various used-book stores. Every year Kevin attends the comic collector's convention, where he buys, sells, and trades. His favorite comics are science-fiction ones. He also likes science-fiction movies.

All of this information had been assembled without any of the Wild Dada Ducks questioning Kevin directly, or drawing any special attention to themselves. We had found all this out by following Kevin, and by engaging various people in casual conversation—working in our questions about Kevin in such a subtle way that nobody ever suspected that we were interested in gathering information about him. Naturally, we were very proud of ourselves. We had gathered quite a lot of highly significant information about our beloved little friend, entirely in secret, and in the space of a little more than twenty-four hours.

"Now," said the Honorable Venustiano Carranza (President of Mexico), "let's discuss what all this data tells us about the lucky lad we have decided to guide and help without his knowledge."

"He leads the most boring life I ever heard of," Igor said.

"There isn't a trace of Dada consciousness in anything he does," Captain Colossal said.

"Except the fat cocker spaniel," I put in.

"Yes," said the Indiana Zephyr, "the fat cocker spaniel has some style, but it isn't really enough to make a Dadaist out of little Kevin, our adopted child."

"I agree," said the Honorable Venustiano Carranza (President of Mexico). "It's hard to tell where to begin helping Kevin Shapiro. The sad truth is, he's evidently a nerd."

"But there's hope," Igor said. "We might be able to rehabilitate him."

"Exactly!" said the Indiana Zephyr. "We have

to do something to shake Kevin out of his dull, normal, un-Dada life-style."

"That will cost you forty cents," said the Honorable Venustiano Carranza (President of Mexico). "Pay each Wild Dada Duck ten cents for saying *life-style*."

There are fines for using certain words—such as life-style. If a Wild Dada Duck should say "Have a nice day," it can cost him five dollars.

The Indiana Zephyr fished out four dimes and handed them around. "Well, you know what I mean," he said.

"Look out! Here comes you-know-who!" Igor said.

Kevin Shapiro had just entered the Balkan Falcon Drug Company. He walked toward the booth where we were sitting. We hadn't seen Kevin Shapiro walking before this. He had a fascinating walk. He sort of bobbed up and down and worked his shoulders as he walked, as though he were listening to music with a bad beat.

Kevin Shapiro came right up to our booth. He stopped walking but continued to hunch his shoulders.

"Quit asking questions about me!" he said.

There was an uncomfortable moment of silence. Finally, the Honorable Venustiano Carranza (President of Mexico) spoke. "You want us to quit doing what?" El Presidente asked, looking puzzled.

"Just quit!" Kevin Shapiro said.

"I assure you, old fellow," Captain Colossal said, "we have no idea what you're talking about."

"I'll punch out your face, see?" Kevin Shapiro said. He shook a pale, skinny fist under the nose of Captain Colossal. "Just quit, that's all."

Kevin Shapiro turned, hunched his shoulders, and bobbed out of the Balkan Falcon Drug Company.

8

"He's a genius!" the Indiana Zephyr said.

"Definitely," Igor said.

"I think he's more than a genius," Captain Colossal said.

"I think he may be God," the Honorable Venustiano Carranza (President of Mexico) said.

"Definitely," I said.

It was clear to the Wild Dada Ducks that Kevin Shapiro had plenty of style, insolence, and punkishness—the raw materials of personal greatness. We loved and admired our adopted boy more than ever.

"We have to do something really wonderful for Kevin Shapiro," the Indiana Zephyr said.

"Yes," said the Honorable Venustiano Carranza (President of Mexico), "nothing is too good for little Kevin. He will inspire our Dada masterpiece."

"But what are we going to do?" I asked.

"How about printing up cards again?" Captain Colossal asked. "They could say *Kevin Shapiro is the greatest.*"

"That's not nearly big enough," said the Indiana Zephyr. "I don't mean to suggest that there's anything wrong with the idea of issuing a Dada card—the Horace Gerstenblut card was a great work of Art—but this is for Kevin. It has to be special."

We all agreed. The Wild Dada Ducks fell silent, chewing the crusts of our raisin toast, all of us trying to think up something magnificent enough to do for Kevin Shapiro.

"We want to call everybody's attention to the fact that Kevin Shapiro is a great person, isn't that right?" I asked.

"Yes," said Igor, "so what's your idea?"

"I don't have an idea yet," I said, "I just wanted to make sure I understood what we're after."

"A person as great as Kevin Shapiro ought to be world famous," El Presidente said.

"That's right!" Captain Colossal said.

"It would be wrong for only us Wild Dada Ducks to know about Kevin Shapiro," Igor said.

"We ought to let the whole world know what a splendid person Kevin Shapiro is," I said.

"Aren't there special guys who work for famous people—movie stars, and politicians, and people like that?" the Indiana Zephyr asked. "You know, they get their names in the paper, and they make sure everybody knows how great they are."

"That's right," I said, "publicity agents, they're called."

"That's it!" the Honorable Venustiano Carranza (President of Mexico) said. "That's what we have to do for little Kevin Shapiro! We have to make him famous and loved by everybody!"

"We'll be his publicity agents!"

"We'll get everybody to appreciate him!"

"We'll make him famous!"

"This is a chance to do something not only for our beloved Kevin Shapiro, but for the whole world!"

"This is a great day for world Dada Culture!"

"So what do we do first?"

"How about printing up a lot of cards?"

"Captain Colossal, can't you think of anything but printing up cards?" the Honorable Venustiano Carranza (President of Mexico) asked.

"Maybe we could print up posters," I said.

"That's it!" everybody said. "A really great poster of Kevin Shapiro—in color."

"We'll print thousands!"

"Everybody will want them!"

"It's perfect!"

"Wait a second!" Igor said. "That will cost a lot of money—probably hundreds. Do we have that much?"

The fact was, the Wild Dada Ducks didn't have any money to speak of. Between us we hardly had hundreds of cents, let alone dollars.

"Isn't that always the way?" the Honorable Venustiano Carranza (President of Mexico) said. "Lack of money once again thwarts a great Artistic enterprise. We'll have to keep thinking."

We kept thinking.

The more we thought, the more the idea of printing up something in the school print shop seemed to have merit. First of all, it didn't cost anything. Captain Colossal could run off the cards almost any day after school, and as long as we were willing to use whatever scrap paper the print shop had lying around, the whole production would be free.

The Honorable Venustiano Carranza (President of Mexico) grumbled quite a bit about printing cards again. He wanted to do something we had never done before. However, since no one including El Presidente could come up with anything that was both good and possible, we finally fell back on Captain Colossal and the printing press. The Honorable Venustiano Carranza (President of Mexico) insisted that we at least make these cards a bit larger than the last batch, and try our best to give them a decent Dada quality. We spent the next hour working on the text for the card. When we finished, and everybody had expressed approval, we gave the final copy to Captain Colossal, with instructions to do his utmost to give the thing an appearance we could all be proud of.

Two days later, in the Balkan Falcon Drug Company, Captain Colossal presented an edition of two thousand cards. They were excellent. Not only was the printing job superior, but the Captain had managed to get some very handsome green cardboard and some printer's cuts showing pictures of this and that which he had artistically arranged to make the cards even more impressive. The whole effect was very fine, and we were all pleased.

KEVIN SHAPIRO
is the
GREATEST Human
Humanoid
Bioelectronic entity
Funky Dude
& Disco Dancer
OF ALL TIME

9

It is funny how fate takes its cut. That is one of the favorite sayings of the Wild Dada Ducks. It means that however carefully you plan things, however much you're sure how things are supposed to turn out—something you never thought of can change everything. Fate will take its cut.

When the Wild Dada Ducks planned and executed the handsome works of Art in honor of Kevin Shapiro, events were already moving in a direction none of us could have guessed. But that is always the way things work. That is why Dada is the greatest Art movement. The Dadaist assumes things are going to go wrong—or at least in an unpredictable direction—so he isn't surprised when it happens. He is surprised when it doesn't.

We distributed the Kevin Shapiro cards in the same manner as the Horace Gerstenblut cards. That is, we left stacks of them in all the bathrooms. Once again we had cause to wish there were some girls in the Duckettes, as darting in and out of the girls' bathrooms was dangerous and scary. However, we got the cards distributed without anyone seeing us, and without meeting anyone apt to get upset.

Because the Wild Dada Ducks are constantly preoccupied with Dada Art and Philosophy, we frequently neglect the events of day-to-day life at Himmler High School. Ask any of us who won the big basketball game last night—and we will ask who was playing. It isn't that we necessarily disapprove of such activities—it's just that you can't lead the way in an Artistic revolution and keep track of every little detail.

So it happened that none of us had the slightest idea that the day we distributed our sincere tribute to Kevin Shapiro was also the day of the Himmler High School Student Council election.

Just as they had done with the Horace Gerstenblut cards, our fellow students picked up the new Kevin Shapiro edition, talked about it, passed cards around to their friends, and tried to guess who Kevin Shapiro might be, and what the cards meant. Of course, that is not the

proper way to appreciate the cards. They are
works of Art to be enjoyed, and experienced—
not analyzed. However, that is not our concern.
As Dada Artists, we provide the Art, the public
can do what it likes with it. Besides, the message of the cards was perfectly obvious. The
cards were intended to notify the world in general, and Himmler High in particular, that
Kevin Shapiro was an exceptionally great human being.

In fact, that part of our message did appear to
have been picked up by a great many people, because, after having a look at the cards, discussing
them, and swapping them around, ninety-seven
percent of the students at Himmler High went
and voted for Kevin Shapiro.

They voted for him for Student Council president, and for all the positions in the Student
Council. All told, Kevin Shapiro received about
28,000 votes from approximately 4,000 students.

We didn't know anything about this, because
the voting was by secret ballot. The results of
the election would be announced in an assembly of the whole school the next day.

The day of the Student Council election was
like any other day in the lives of the Wild Dada
Ducks. We had executed our Artwork, we went
to our classes, we picked up ballots for the Student Council election, and each voted for Kevin
Shapiro for all seven places, including Student
Council president.

47

At the assembly the following day the official candidates for office were all lined up, sitting in a row on folding chairs on the auditorium stage. They were wearing suits and dresses. They had sat in the same order, wearing the same outfits, the week before, when each candidate had made a campaign speech.

Mr. Gerstenblut, the vice-principal, and Mr. Winter, the principal, were both on stage too. Mr. Winter made a short speech about how we were lucky to live in a democracy and be able to vote in elections, and the usual stuff they tell you at school elections. The Wild Dada Ducks have nothing against democracy, except that it doesn't go nearly far enough—but the thing about being elected to a school office that we find boring is that you wouldn't get to pass any real laws even if you got elected.

Miss Steele, the chairman of the election committee, came out to read the results of the tabulation of all the votes.

"We have a very remarkable situation here," Miss Steele said. "It seems there have been a great many write-in votes for a candidate who hadn't even announced that he was in the race. Now, ordinarily, the election committee would insist on the rule that states that if a candidate for Student Council president is not one of those duly nominated, votes for that person will be discounted. The rule further states that if the person with the winning number of votes is not one of those duly nominated, the duly nominated person with the next largest number of votes will be elected. However, in this election one extremely popular young man has gotten practically all the votes, for all the offices on the Student Council—and, as you may have guessed, he is not one of those duly nominated.

"The committee feels that it will be best if we declare the election as having miscarried," Miss Steele went on, to considerable booing. "We are going to hold another election, by show of hands, here this morning—but in the interest of fairness, we would like to invite the young man who got so many votes to come up on the stage and say a few words. You've already heard from the other fine candidates. Now, will the young man who has already demonstrated that he has the confidence of his fellow students please approach the stage? Will Kevin Shapiro please come up and say a few words?"

There was a thunderous outburst of applause. There was also a good deal of neck-craning and looking around, since almost nobody in the school knew who Kevin Shapiro was.

From the very last row in the auditorium a small, thin figure shuffled and bobbed down the aisle, and then bounded up the steps to the stage. It was our boy. It was Kevin Shapiro. The Wild Dada Ducks started a cheer that was wildly taken up by everyone else in the school. Kevin Shapiro, cool as you please, stood on the stage, waiting for the cheering and clapping to die down. I noticed for the first time that Kevin had these really klutzy shoes. They looked like Frankenstein boots. I think he picked shoes with the thickest possible soles, in an attempt to get an extra inch of height. The shoes made Kevin Shapiro look incredibly Dada. He shifted from foot to foot and waited for the crowd to be quiet.

Finally the last whistle and foot-stomp and cheer had echoed through the auditorium, and Kevin Shapiro spoke.

"Hey," he said, "I don't want to be any slob president of the Student Council. Don't vote for me, see? Vote for these idiots here."

The applause was deafening. It went on for about ten minutes.

Kevin was reelected by a landslide.

10

The Wild Dada Ducks were filled with pride and delight. In just one short day following our public expression of appreciation, Kevin Shapiro had been almost unanimously recognized as the finest example of humanity in the whole school. The crowd in the auditorium was going crazy. The cheering had consolidated into a continuous roar, as Kevin Shapiro, now elected for the second time—this time by acclamation—approached the microphone.

It took a long time for the audience to become quiet. Kevin Shapiro, who appeared to us to be a born public speaker and leader of men, patiently waited until the last expression of enthusiasm had been uttered. He held up both hands in a gesture for silence, which was at the same time friendly, endearing. Kevin Shapiro was the most beloved person in all of Himmler High School at that moment.

"Look," he began, "I thought I made myself clear. I do not want to be on your stupid Student Council. Just leave me alone. Anybody bothers me, I'll bash his face in, see?" Kevin shook a fist meaningfully, and returned to his seat.

There was another spontaneous demonstration of support for Kevin Shapiro but no amount of cheering and chanting could induce him to leave his auditorium seat and speak to the students again. The crowd showed no sign of leaving peaceably, and finally Mr. Winter, who has an astonishingly loud voice, took over.

Mr. Winter declared the day's exercises over, and by executive order abolished all elections in the school until further notice.

This is why the Wild Dada Ducks—and apparently Kevin Shapiro—do not take school elections seriously. Mr. Winter has the last word.

The crowd left the auditorium in an ugly mood. Every teacher in Himmler High knew that the rest of the day was going to be grim. There was a lot of resentment expressed toward Mr. Winter for abolishing elections, and his resentment extended to all figures of authority, especially teachers.

Somehow, nobody seemed to be angry at little Kevin Shapiro. He had twice rejected the nearly unanimous vote of the entire student body—and in no uncertain terms. He had called them stupid, and made it plain that he couldn't be bothered to serve as Student Council president. And yet, no one appeared to have taken offense. The students of Himmler High School respected Kevin's wish, and mostly left him alone. It was really unheard-of behavior. I mean, the majority of the students are far from being philosophers, let alone Dadaists. To tell the truth, most of the kids are only human on a technicality. They take great mindless pride in their school—they go to all the games and scream bloody murder—about once every other year there is a mass fistfight with the students from Kissinger High School, our great rival.

Now, Kevin Shapiro, a little, skinny, bespectacled kid, had openly rejected one of the institutions of Himmler High. In effect he had rejected the whole population of the school—and nobody tried to kill him! The only thing the Wild Dada Ducks could make of this remarkable behavior was that, like us, simply anybody who saw Kevin Shapiro could not help loving him. Captain Colossal said he had charisma. Igor said it was star quality. Whatever it was, Kevin definitely had it, and we were all very proud of him. We were ashamed to remember that up until the last minute, we were all going to vote for the Marquis de Sade.

11

Of course, school elections, and assemblies, and all of those things are dumb. Anyone would realize it if it were given any thought—but generally, nobody thinks about those things. The Wild Dada Ducks do not approve of school elections, naturally, because we are for the abolishment of government as we know it. We want the machines to take over. That is, we want ordinary, loyal, everyday machines, like dishwashers and buses and pencil sharpeners, to take over the government—not computers and robots, which are probably really in charge already. The Wild Dada Ducks do not approve of school elections, but the ordinary unenlightened Himmler High School students just love them.

At least that's what we thought until the election of Kevin Shapiro (who refused to serve). To tell the truth, we weren't sure what was going through the minds of our fellow students. Mostly, we were proud of how popular our boy, Kevin Shapiro, had become because of the distribution of our Dada card. We didn't consider what might be the innermost thoughts of the other kids in the school.

Later we got an idea of what the whole school thought of Kevin Shapiro.

They worshipped him.

Kevin was the single biggest hero in the school. He was the only hero in the school. In a single moment he had expressed the secret truth about school elections, the school, the world, being a kid—everything. Every kid in the auditorium that day realized the reality of his situation when Kevin Shapiro said that he didn't want to be on any stupid Student Council. Most kids wouldn't have said anything like that, even if they were thinking it—but Kevin did.

Like the Wild Dada Ducks, every kid in the school had realized that Kevin Shapiro had a style all his own. Just as we had predicted, he was a natural leader.

Kevin's wish that he be left alone only made everybody love and respect him more. All the girls were in love with him. All the boys were afraid of him. Simply anybody would have died of happiness if Kevin Shapiro had smiled at them, or winked, or spoken, or anything.

All this was true, but nobody actually realized it—or realized the extent or importance of it. When we filed out of the auditorium that day, nobody was conscious of the great event that had taken place—with the possible exception of Mr. Winter and Mr. Gerstenblut, both of whom looked worried. They had taken courses in being a principal, and they knew they had the makings of an uprising on their hands. They knew this, or they may have known it—but there was nothing they could do but wait.

The Wild Dada Ducks were not worried, even when Kevin Shapiro passed by us in the crush of people leaving the auditorium. He smiled a grim smile, and rubbed his belly, as if he were thinking about something good to eat. "I'll get you for this," he said.

We just attributed his remark and gesture to his natural charm, and were even a little flattered that he had spoken to us. We didn't understand that Kevin Shapiro was the king of the school—and we didn't understand the power a king has.

Everything appeared to go back to normal at once. As far as the Wild Dada Ducks were concerned, the election and the assembly in the auditorium were part of the Dada Work we had started with the cards—and it had been our most successful exercise so far. Now it was over, and we all felt good about it.

12

Nothing changed at first. The day after the Student Council elections, and the day after that, life at Himmler High School was normal, average. Students went from class to class, the Wild Dada Ducks met to discuss Art and Culture in the Balkan Falcon Drug Company, and Kevin Shapiro ate alone in the lunchroom. Mr. Winter and Mr. Gerstenblut appeared in the halls very often, looking alert and nervous, as though they expected to find something important going on—but nothing was going on.

That's what they thought.

That's what we thought.

That's what everyone thought.

It was on the third day after the election that the Fanatical Praetorians first appeared. We didn't know they were the Fanatical Praetorians at first. They were all the kids in Himmler High who were shorter than Kevin Shapiro, and they all had sailor hats.

These sailor hats were of the variety worn by Donald Duck in the early cartoons. They were soft and white, with a ribbon hanging down in the back. I don't know where they got them. There was a blue band around the bottom of the hats with the words *S.S. Popnick* printed in white. They must have been navy surplus, but from which country's navy, I don't know.

The short kids in sailor/duck hats all sat in the lunchroom, not too close to Kevin Shapiro, but surrounding him on all sides. They all ate Grape-Nuts from little cartons into which they had poured milk. Most of them had big Frankenstein shoes like Kevin Shapiro. All of them had sworn an oath to protect Kevin with their lives.

Kevin Shapiro had recruited the Fanatical Praetorians, and administered the oath. Not only had he organized a bodyguard, and, as we gradually learned—an illegal government within the school—Kevin Shapiro had also started an Art Movement.

It was called Heroic Realism.

We didn't find all these things out at once. At first, all we knew was that a bunch of little kids in sailor hats were trailing around a respectful distance behind Kevin Shapiro, and if anyone approached him or tried to talk to him, they would make a wall of their bodies and threaten the person who intended to approach.

Since Kevin Shapiro didn't like to talk to people, and mostly wanted to be left alone, there weren't many confrontations with the Fanatic Praetorians. It seemed a little weird, and that was all.

Then came Heroic Realism. As we had found out when we were doing research about him, Kevin Shapiro was a big comic-book fan. It turned out that what he liked best about comic books was the artwork. The Wild Dada Ducks had declared comic books unartistic a long time ago. Not only did we find the stories predictable and boring, but the pictures seemed particularly awful to us. For the most part, they showed guys with too many muscles and heads too small for their bodies.

Kevin Shapiro loved comic books.

Heroic Realism declared that anything that wasn't a comic book was no good. Anybody who didn't like comic books was no good. Conversely, anybody who liked comic books was a great person. That, as far as we could make out, was all there was to Heroic Realism.

Every student in Himmler High was a Heroic Realist. Except us, of course. Also, every student in Himmler High recognized Kevin Shapiro as his supreme leader.

Kevin Shapiro was a good deal more than

president of the Student Council. It was obvious why he had scorned that basically meaningless honor. Kevin Shapiro had become undisputed king of Himmler High. His word was law. Of course, he practically never said anything, but if he had said anything, it would have been law.

Obviously, he communicated to the Fanatical Praetorians. If Kevin Shapiro wanted to tell anybody anything, it was done through the Fanatical Praetorians. For example, if you were sitting in the lunchroom, a half-dozen Fanatical Praetorians might come over to you and say, "Kevin doesn't want you sitting there." So you'd move. Everybody was afraid of the Fanatical Praetorians.

They were little, but there were a lot of them. Also, they had learned to imitate Kevin's special way of being persuasive. "Look," they'd say, "we'll punch out your face, see?" It never failed to get results.

Big kids, who had formerly been known as bullies, cowered and cringed before the short kids in the Donald Duck hats. Some kids wanted to become Fanatical Praetorians, but they weren't short enough.

After school every day Kevin Shapiro would be escorted away from the school by a big crowd of Fanatical Praetorians. They even guarded him on weekends. Once I saw him leafing through comic books in a store downtown while ten or eleven shrimps in sailor hats stood around him.

After a week or two everybody was sufficiently afraid of the Fanatical Praetorians that they were obeyed even when they were alone. Even the teachers learned to respect them. In the biology class taken by the Indiana Zephyr and Captain Colossal, there was only one Fanatical Praetorian, a kid named Shep Stoneman. It seems Shep Stoneman got into an argument with the teacher. The teacher wanted Shep to remove his sailor hat. Shep didn't want to. Finally, Shep told the entire class to get up and leave the room. They did it.

Mr. Winter and Mr. Gerstenblut were all over the building dealing with problems caused by the Fanatical Praetorians. There were a great many comic books being circulated in the school because of the Heroic Realism movement, and there had been a number of tense moments between teachers and Fanatical Praetorians.

At one point Mr. Winter outlawed the wearing of hats in school. The next day, by order of the Fanatical Praetorians, every kid in the school wore a hat of some kind all day, and a general strike was threatened. That is, all the kids wore hats except the Wild Dada Ducks.

This constituted a moral dilemma for us. Here was the breakdown of the normal un-Dada order, which we had all wished for, but we found we couldn't go along with the hats-on or-

der which emanated from Kevin Shapiro—a
hero we ourselves had created. We didn't exactly know why we felt we could not go along
with it. There was something about Heroic Realism that made it impossible—but it was more
than that. We had been nonconformists for so
long that it just didn't feel right to go along with
everyone else—and there was something else,
too, but we couldn't say what it was.

Of course, the hat-wearing was a complete
success. What could Mr. Winter do? He couldn't
very well call in the police. Nobody was doing
anything destructive—they were wearing hats,
that was all. He couldn't suspend everybody. He
couldn't very well write to everyone's parents
and say that little Johnny had worn a hat on
such-and-such a day and was therefore suspended. It was a clear victory for Kevin and his
loyal followers. That was everybody but the
Wild Dada Ducks.

Mr. Winter wriggled out of his defeat, un-
gracefully, by having all the homeroom teachers read something about how styles change,
and how Himmler High students have always
been models of good grooming and acceptable
dress, and that if hats were "in" then the administration of the school wasn't about to spoil
anybody's fun, and how Mr. Winter always kept
up with the times, and had even personally been
to a disco with his wife, and sometimes didn't
wear a necktie.

It didn't fool anybody. The Fanatical Praetorians were running the place, and they obeyed nobody but Kevin Shapiro. It only remained to see what Kevin would decide to do next.

13

The Wild Dada Ducks were especially interested in what Kevin Shapiro would do next. Obviously, it had not gone unnoticed that we had
been the only ones not to wear hats during the
protest. The truth was, we were somewhat
afraid of what the Fanatical Praetorians might
do to us. One thing was certain—they would not
do anything except on Kevin Shapiro's order.

The next thing Kevin Shapiro got interested
in was making sure that everybody in the school
ate Grape-Nuts. This project interested him so
much that he actually spoke to the assembled
kids in the lunchroom one day.

Kevin got up and struck a pose indicating that

he was about to speak. Even without the shushing and fingers to lips of the Fanatical Praetorians, the room would have fallen silent in a hurry. This was to be the first public utterance of Kevin Shapiro since he had turned down the Student Council.

"Grape-Nuts is good!" he said.

After that no lunch at Himmler High School did not include a little carton of Grape-Nuts cereal with milk poured into the waxed paper liner. The school lunchroom didn't have enough in stock at first, and kids brought Grape-Nuts from home. Lunchtime became a symphony of crunching and slurping.

Fearing for our lives, and arguing that as Dadaists we had already approved of Grape-Nuts, the Wild Dada Ducks joined in the cereal-eating. Secretly, we hoped that our failure to wear hats that day when everybody else wore them might be forgotten, especially since we were eating Grape-Nuts like the Heroic Realists.

And in fact, it seemed that our act of disloyalty had been forgotten. In the days that followed, nothing special happened. Of course, the fulminations of the Heroic Realists annoyed us no end. Kids went on and on about the beauty of comic books, and our Dada sensibilities were continually offended by snatches of overheard conversation about Mouse-Man and Wonder Wombat—but in general, life was bearable at Himmler High School.

Kevin Shapiro's main concern seemed to be

the continued eating of Grape-Nuts. Often at lunchtime he could be seen contentedly surveying the spectacle of a great many kids, all working away at their little boxes of cereal.

The lunchroom at Himmler High is large, as is the school itself. While the room is not capable of containing the whole student population, a good thousand can eat there at once. Nowadays, they ate a good thousand boxes of Grape-Nuts at once.

Kevin Shapiro's concern about the cerealeating was such that he actually spoke again. This time he climbed up onto a table and gestured for silence.

"Get 'em good and soggy," he said.

After this, people took considerably longer with their lunches. Under the ever-watchful eye of Kevin and his bodyguard, it became customary to let the milk and cereal sit uneaten for ten or fifteen minutes, the Grape-Nuts absorbing all the milk that did not run out the corners of the carton.

One day, a deputation of Fanatical Praetorians actually walked around the lunchroom, inspecting people's Grape-Nuts to see that they were good and soggy.

A couple of days after the Praetorian tour of inspection, Kevin Shapiro once again, and for the last time, addressed the assembled lunching students.

Again he stood upon a table, not too far from where the Wild Dada Ducks were sitting. He had his carton of well-sogged Grape-Nuts in his hand.

"Look!" said Kevin Shapiro. "Watch me!"

Kevin Shapiro turned the box over and dumped the soggy contents into his cupped right hand.

"Down with Dada!" he shouted, and hurled the mess of dripping Grape-Nuts right into the face of the Honorable Venustiano Carranza (President of Mexico).

What followed was horrible. The Wild Dada Ducks were served at least one thousand portions of Grape-Nuts. They were thrown at us, poured over our heads, stuffed down our pants, and mushed into our hair. The massacre took place so quickly that we never had time to get out of our chairs. We sat there, stunned, and were turned into living, dripping statues.

When we left the lunchroom we squished as we walked, and left a sloppy trail of cereal.

14

Not long after the Grape-Nuts devastation, it seems Kevin Shapiro disbanded the invincible Fanatical Praetorians. Heroic Realism appeared to wane as an Art Movement, and conditions at the school returned entirely to normal.

Kevin Shapiro, refusing to do anything to exploit the total power he had over his fellow students, was gradually forgotten, and could be seen hunched over his Grape-Nuts at lunch, alone as before.

When he saw any of the Wild Dada Ducks he laughed to himself.

The Wild Dada Ducks left him alone.

We also suspended our program of cultural improvement for our fellow students. We continued to meet after school every day in the Balkan Falcon Drug Company. There we pursued our discussions of Art and Philosophy.

For about a week we made no mention of our experience in the lunchroom with the Grape-Nuts. Finally, it seemed time to discuss its implications and historical importance.

"Does it seem possible," asked Igor, "that Kevin Shapiro seized control of the entire school just so he could have us covered with wet breakfast cereal?"

No one was sure. It could have been planned from the start, or it could have just been an idea that occurred to him at the moment.

"The important question," said Captain Colossal, "is what is the significance of Kevin's rise to power, and the Grape-Nuts attack? What does it mean in philosophical terms?"

"Yes," said the Indiana Zephyr, "what is the moral of the story?"

"It has no moral," said the Honorable Venustiano Carranza (President of Mexico), "it is a Dada story."

Dead End
Dada

Dedicated
to the spirit of

LIEUTENANT HIROO ONADA

who hid on the Philippine island of Lubang for over thirty-four years—until February 20, 1979—not knowing that World War II had ended

Mutato nomine de te fabula narratur—

From the author . . .

Following the publication of my book, *Young Adult Novel*, in 1982, I began to receive, by mail, additional chapters of the story-within-a-story, *Kevin Shapiro, Boy Orphan*. All of these submissions have been anonymous, or obviously pseudonymous. The letters bear postmarks from various parts of the country. I do not pretend to understand the motivation of the authors of these works; however, I take the opportunity afforded by the publication of this present volume to include a few of these curious contributions:

Kevin Shapiro
Chapter number 9,485

Kevin had heard about food poisoning, but he never thought that something this bad could ever happen. All the kids at his birthday party dead, and all because of that cake mix with the slightly bitter smell! The first birthday of his life that he'd had a party. He had been so happy! Now, disaster. As he looked at the seven little corpses all slumped in their seats, party hats still in place, he wondered, What will I tell their mothers? Will I get to keep the presents? How will I explain about the fiery angel that warned only me to eat nothing?

With a resigned air he reached for the cake cutter.

I judge the selection cited above to be an authentic if above-average example of junior high school composition (as are all that follow), even though the author spelled *fiery* correctly, which I never do.

Kevin Shapiro
Chapter number 7,217

There Kevin stood with the ax. The ax that only yesterday had slipped from his father's hands to slice his own leg in two. And there was the puddle of blood that had thrown Kevin's mother into a hysterical frenzy, causing her to thrust both her hands down the garbage disposal while it was on. Kevin knew that if his mother hadn't done that his father would have been taken to the hospital in time. Kevin called the ambulance, but by the time they arrived both parents had been deprived of oxygen for too long. Of course they could be saved, but all of their limbs would have to be amputated and their total IQ would never exceed 42.

Although Kevin was out shooting kittens with his rifle while it happened, he knew it was all his fault as he ate a box of rat poison and slowly passed away in the front yard.

I take this to be the work of the writer of the birthday party episode cited above. The number 42 may be significant.

Kevin Shapiro
Chapter number 3,279.741

Kevin had been walking through the desert for two weeks now, and his body had emaciated away to 48 pounds, and all the hair had fallen out of his head.

The drone of the plane caused him to look toward the heavens. There it was! The rescue plane!

An object was dropped, with the white parachute billowing open. Running over to receive the rescue package, Kevin tripped over a cow skull, twisting his knee, leaving himself immobilized. He then proceeded to be crushed by his chance for life.

The work of another hand. On the same page, another Kevin Shapiro chapter is indicated with the number 4,732.17401; however, there is no further text as such. Instead, there are two stylized heads labeled "The Mad Artist Strikes the Red Army" and "The Mad Artist's Partner Strikes for Higher Wages." I have no hint of what these may mean.

Kevin Shipiro [sic]   Ch. 1,476

"Why me? Don't blame me. It was just a game—only tag. I didn't mean to push her down the stairs," wheezed Kevin to his guidance counselor.

Kevin's sister was finally home. Not drunk, stoned, or pregnant like the other times. Playing happily, they ran around the upstairs until Kevin's playful shove sent his sister tumbling.

In an uncontrollable rage his mother rushed at Kevin, but tripped over the coffee table and thwacked her head on the hearth, sending her into an endless sleep.

By "Jimmy Burrito." There are some other submissions, in a different hand, with the same misspelling of the name Shapiro. Record as to whether

the "Shipiro" contributions come from the same lo-
cality has unfortunately been lost.

Kevin Shipiro, Boy Orphan
(no chapter number)

Kevin Shipiro thought about jumping off the
ledge. He had had a rotten life. In fact it was so
rotten that it nauseated him to think about it.
Kevin didn't really want to jump, but the people below kept chanting, "Jump! Jump!" Kevin
decided not to jump. While edging his way to
the window, Kevin slipped and took out three
of the crowd.

Orthographic differences suggest that this is not
the work of the author of the example cited previ-
ously, though the misspelling of Shapiro and some
stylistic elements are similar.

Kevin Shapiro, Boy Orphan
Episode number 560½

The old woman stopped at the curb, feeling its sloping inclination with the tip of her
cane. "DON'T WALK!" flashed the light—then
"WALK!" in a friendly green. The puce Volvo
making a right turn on red did not look friendly,
nor did the blaring taxi, or any of the other obnoxious vehicles.

If only little Kevin would come. . . . For weeks he'd been helping her across Reynolds Avenue at that most ghastly of all intersections, but how long would he last, facing adversity again and again in the name of helping-grannies-type Americana? Would he help, or had insanity finally claimed him as her own?

. . . He whipped out a paperback book and screamed, "I am Charles the Cat!" Obviously, he had been driven to the brink. Long days working in the glue factory feeding live horses into the pulverizer had scarred his psyche. Yes, he had tried seeking psychiatric help, but the shrink had accomplished nothing except making Kevin a heroin addict. Since the doctor was also a perverted, sexually depraved, sadomasochistic, bisexual child molester, he had taken advantage of Kevin. Now, wracked with syphilis, Kevin moved toward Granny Mulohan. Could he bear to help another human in trouble, besieged as he was by his own little tragedies?

The orphanage had threatened to evict him if he was late again, and he always was late when he helped the old dear. As it was, he'd eaten nothing but dog food for a week, that being the customary punishment for tardiness.

"Kevin?" Her dim blue eyes tried to focus on him.

"Kevin?" Mrs. Mulohan waited in confusion.

It was too much. Kevin took out a loofah and sloughed himself to death.

* * *

The writer of this chapter, in a postscript, identifies herself as a female.

Kevin Shapiro   Number 87-3659

Kevin was sitting in the principal's office feeling miserable. It wasn't his fault. He didn't belong here.

Yesterday Kevin's teacher had given the class an assignment due the next day. When the rest of the class, except for Kevin, turned one in the teacher became upset and ordered Kevin down to the office.

The principal motioned for Kevin to come into his office, and Kevin obediently obeyed. "It says here that you refused to do the homework," read the principal. "Is this true?"

"I just couldn't do it," pleaded Kevin.

"Why couldn't you write an essay on the happiest moment of your life?"

"I haven't had any."

Serious students, educators, members of official law-enforcement organizations, and the morbidly curious, having convinced me that their interest is sincere, may apply through the publisher for photocopied facsimiles of the compositions cited here, and numerous others.

I have included the examples for purposes of general edification, and to demonstrate that while the esteemed community which devotes itself to criticism of juvenile literature declared *Young Adult Novel* (to which this is a sister volume) to be an outrage of various sorts—it has typically fallen wide of the mark in assessing the damage it might do.

It is this author's devout hope that in time he may be able to produce acceptable books about cute furry animals and—for the older reader—stories about high schools in California with really good athletic programs and uniformly attractive students. In the meantime, while the sort of adumbrated and sinister production which follows these remarks continues to issue forth (to my considerable enrichment—and the publisher's), the least I can do is to entreat teachers and librarians of the better sort to keep the book out of the hands of the young.

I

Decay is inevitable in all compound things.
Work out your own salvation with the utmost
  diligence.

—G. Buddha

Nuclear destruction is inevitable.

Did you know that some of the most powerful men in this country—leaders of the military, industry, and politics—go away to this fancy mansion and play games, like squirting each other with shaving cream, having water fights, and looking at porn movies, and all sorts of practical jokes involving the bathroom?

Any number of professional prostitutes have gone on record to the effect that their weirdest clients—the ones who need to get dressed up in chicken suits, and so forth—are prominent people in politics.

These are the people who run everything. Do they seem competent to you? Do you know that in the recent past we had two presidents of the United States in a row whose favorite lunch was cottage cheese with catsup on it? Do you know who the president of the United States is as you read this? Do you know what he eats for lunch?

These are the people in charge of the nuclear arsenal. I ask the reader—is there any reason to believe that these idiots will fail to blow up the world?

The answer is: Only by accident will the present power elite, in this country and others, fail to blow up the world.

Is there any hope? There is only this: The people under discussion tend to do most things by accident.

It was the realization of these facts that led the Wild Dada Ducks to the further realization that our position as Dadaists was no longer correct. For one thing, being Dadaists—compared for example with the behavior of world leaders—actually made sense. This put us out of harmony with the universe—that is to say our aesthetic and artistic position was out of harmony. Our position in society—that of high school students—was as ridiculous as ever.

The Wild Dada Ducks held a solemn council. Our leader, the Honorable Venustiano Carranza (President of Mexico) explained to us that Earth is doomed. We removed our eyeglasses and observed forty-two seconds of silence in memory of our beautiful planet. Igor, who does not wear eyeglasses, removed his socks. It was a touching moment.

The matter of our world's impending destruction was considered, and it was decided that as socially responsible Wild Dada Ducks, we must take decisive action.

The first thing we agreed on was that the Wild Dada Ducks ought to anticipate the end of everything by ceasing to exist ourselves. This was unanimously agreed upon, and we instantly became the former Wild Dada Ducks.

The Wild Dada Ducks had been the five most brilliant and progressive students at Himmler High School. It was a great blow to world culture when we went out of existence. Our former leader had been the Honorable Venustiano Carranza (President of Mexico). The other members were the Indiana Zephyr; Igor, who did not wear glasses; Captain Colossal; and myself, Charles the Cat. Our former goal had been to promote world Dada consciousness. To this end we had put forth many amazing and wonderful Dada works of Art. We had placed a beautiful high-tech toilet in the trophy case of Himmler High School. We had distributed copies of our Dada Manifesto, and had ruled Horace Gerstenblut out of existence by publication of the dreaded N'EXISTE PAS card. We had written and performed Dada plays, and had unwittingly invented the dictator Kevin Shapiro and elevated him to absolute power. These things, with the possible exception of Kevin Shapiro's reign of terror, all brought credit to ideas which exemplified Dada.

In view of the emergency that faced the world, we had agreed that we must sadly abandon our work in favor of Dada consciousness, and address ourselves to the question of discovering whether consciousness exists in any form at all.

"This is no time to be particular," said our beloved leader, the Honorable Venustiano Carranza (President of Mexico).

The reason that we had not removed our hats as a gesture of respect for the fate of the world was that we, who were once Wild Dada Ducks, did not wear hats as a sign of our status as freethinkers.

Having caused ourselves to cease to exist as Wild Dada Ducks, it remained for us to alter our philosophy, become more energetic, and to reconstitute ourselves as a new and more dynamic entity. We also felt that it was time to abandon the logic, reasonableness, and rationality that had characterized all our activities as Dadaists. We needed to transcend logic, which had brought the human race to such a pitiful condition.

It was the Indiana Zephyr who introduced the historic course which we were to take—that which would give a more appropriate connotation to our activities henceforth. The Indiana Zephyr suggested that instead of Dada as our guiding principle, we should all embrace Zen.

This was really brilliant. We could all tell that our leader, the Honorable Venustiano Carranza (President of Mexico), was wishing he had thought of it. We instantly saw that this was the appropriate course of action, and unanimously agreed to make Zen the cornerstone of our lives from that moment forward.

"Just one question," Igor said after the cheering and handshaking. "Just what is Zen?"

"I'm not entirely sure," said the Indiana Zephyr.

"There's just time to get to the library before it closes," Captain Colossal said.

We ran all the way.

II
Ex libris

The librarian told us that we were six or seven years too late. The library had removed all the Zen books from circulation because nobody checked them out anymore.

The only thing the Wild Dada Ducks could find on the topic was a book about Zen Cookery. We checked it out and took it with us.

The next item on the agenda was to issue a statement. We composed the statement, leafing through the Zen cookbook for inspiration as we walked.

The statement:

Henceforth we shall be known as the Dharma Ducks, formerly the Wild Dada Ducks, and also as the Wild Zen Dada Ducks. We are now working for a world cultural revolution, the destruction of authority, freedom for all oppressed peoples, and sex with the junior and senior girls, all of them if possible. So far we have failed in our goals, especially the last, but we carry on. We are ready. SEMPER PARATUS. We carry condoms in our wallets and look for chances to promote world revolution all the time.

Is it our fault if the forces of repression have constantly foiled us? We are sincere. It was hard enough when we were Dadaists—but now as Zens we are misunderstood and reviled even by ourselves.

The single event which caused our beloved leader, El Presidente, to realize that all was lost and mankind doomed was the destruction of our meeting place, the Balkan Falcon Drug Company. It was torn down. In its place, in a very few weeks, a mini-strip-mall was created. There was a self-service laundry on the spot where the Balkan Falcon Drug Company once had stood. The self-service laundry had a coffee machine, and chairs—and although it was nothing like the Balkan Falcon Drug Company, the Dharma Ducks, or Wild Zen Dada Ducks as we are also officially known, loyally use it as a meeting place. However, we shall never forget our sense of shock and disappointment at the destruction of our good old Balkan Falcon—and have always referred to the laundry as the Balkan Falcon Memorial Laundromat.

As a gesture of our despair and defiance—and in order to make the proprietor of the self-service laundry like us, so that he would let us use the place—the Wild Zen Dada Ducks pretended to like country and western music, and encouraged the owner of the Balkan Falcon Memorial Laundromat, Sigmund Yee, to play the radio—which he was always playing anyway—louder.

III

The best kind of student is like the best kind of horse—it runs when it sees only the shadow of the whip.

—Gautama Sakyamuni

Having nothing but a cookery book to inform us constituted a slight handicap for the Dharma Ducks. However, we were able to extrapolate, as the Indiana Zephyr said.

We sat in the uncomfortable plastic chairs in the Balkan Falcon Memorial Laundromat and studied the book.

The first significant clue was espied by Igor. "These recipes are not eatable!" he said.

We saw that it was true. The recipes called for things like thin soy sauce, seaweed of various kinds, brown rice, gluten noodles, plus some roots and tubers none of us had ever heard of. The illustrations made it clear that there was nothing in the book a human being could eat.

"He's right," I said, looking at a recipe for brown rice and aduki bean pudding (the other ingredient was soy sauce), "no human would willingly eat this."

"I would eat it," said Captain Colossal.

"Which further proves what Charles the Cat just said," remarked the Honorable Venustiano Carranza (President of Mexico). "The Captain is notably unhuman in his eating habits."

"Here's another," Igor said. "Boiled rice cream. The ingredients are rice cream powder, boiling water, and a quarter teaspoon of oil."

"Sounds like paste," El Presidente said.

"I'd probably eat it," said Captain Colossal.

"I think this book is trying to tell us something," said the Indiana Zephyr.

"I think this book is trying to make us sick," I said.

"You want to hear about pan-fried brown rice croquettes?" Igor asked.

"What's in it?" El Presidente asked.

"Brown rice, rice cream cereal, and rice flour."

"I might eat that—if I could put something on it, like mayonnaise," the Captain said.

"You put soy sauce on it," Igor said.

"I might not eat it," said Captain Colossal.

"This book is definitely trying to tell us something," the Indiana Zephyr said.

"I agree," said the Honorable Venustiano Carranza (President of Mexico), "it's clear that it isn't a cookbook as such. There must be some deep and secret message. Somebody read the introduction—see if there's a clue there."

The introduction was written by Ms. Wakamae Weinberg, the author of *The Official Zen Cookery Book*. In the beginning she talked about how there are principles of positive and negative—called yin and yang—in all things, especially food. The idea is to have five parts yin-type food to one part yang-type food in everything you eat. It wasn't clear how a dish like pan-fried rice croquettes could be divided into yin and yang, being made of nothing but rice—but we read on, looking for the secret message.

Then Wakamae Weinberg went on to talk about her great teacher, Alan W. Watzuki, the inventor of Zen-yin-yang, the system of cooking on which the book was based. Alan W. Watzuki had died of gastroenteritis in Bucharest, Romania, at a relatively early age, leaving his followers to carry on the work as best they could. She said that the most important thing in learning about Zen is to find a Zen master.

"This might be what we're looking for," said

the Honorable Venustiano Carranza (President of Mexico).

Wakamae Weinberg said that the best kind of Zen master comes from Asia. You can tell that he's a Zen master by his concentrated expression and inexplicable, even strange behavior. He should have a unique expression in his eyes, and should be orderly and intent in his work. The very best Zen masters always have fat feet. When one approaches a true Zen master, he will invariably deny that he knows anything about Zen—maybe even becoming angry and excited. This is a sure sign of a really high quality Zen master.

The serious student of Zen must not expect the Zen master to take him by the hand and show him things. It is up to the student to figure out what the Zen master wants him to do.

Wakamae Weinberg then went on to tell her own experiences as the pupil of the incomparable Zen-yin-yang master, Alan W. Watzuki. By certain unmistakable indications, she realized that Watzuki wanted her to carve a perfect replica of a 1977 Volkswagen Rabbit out of a potato. When she brought him her first attempt, Watzuki threw the potato against the wall, smashing it. Wakamae Weinberg was destroyed by the experience—but she persevered. She brought him another potato carved into a Volkswagen, and this time Watzuki took it from her and mashed it into a pulp with his hair-brush. Then he made her pay for a new hair-brush because his was now all messed up.

After a while she lost count of how many times she had carved a potato into a Volks-wagen Rabbit. Every time, Watzuki rejected the carving. At last, in a state of perfect mindless-ness, she carved a potato into a Volkswagen Rabbit convertible, with the top down. When she brought this to Watzuki he smiled, and at that moment Wakamae Weinberg experienced enlightenment.

"Wow!" the Indiana Zephyr said.

"Sounds great," Captain Colossal said.

"What would have happened if she'd carved the convertible first?" Igor asked.

"The point is, where are we going to find a Zen master?" the Honorable Venustiano Car-ranza (President of Mexico) asked.

We sat in the Balkan Falcon Memorial Laun-dromat, wishing we knew where to find a Zen master. The owner of the Laundromat, Sig-mund Yee, was methodically stacking nickels, dimes, and quarters on the shelf that ran above the row of washing machines. He stared at the coins with an intent expression, and counted under his breath. The radio was blaring a cow-boy song about being all alone on the trail. Sig-mund Yee occasionally took a spoonful of blueberry yogurt from a container on the shelf.

The Dharma Ducks all noticed him at once.

"Could it possibly be?" the Indiana Zephyr asked.

"Look at his feet!" Igor whispered.

We looked at Master Yee's feet. They were fat—plenty fat. Fatter than any feet we had ever seen. The truth is, Master Yee was good and fat all over. He was trying to reduce—hence the yogurt, instead of the double bean burritos he usually munched in his Laundromat.

"How about that look in his eyes?" Captain Colossal whispered.

"It's unique," I said.

"Master," El Presidente said out loud.

"Master," Igor said.

"Master," we all said.

Master Yee turned toward us. "Now you make fun of me, huh?" he said. "Not enough you sloppy kids sit all time in laundry, drink coffee, smoke cigarettes, take up space—Yee lets you hang, hang around alla time, now you start in make stupid remarks? You think Yee talk funny, prob'ly, little racist bastards! You get out! Get out, punks! I shove this yogurt in you face, little bastards!"

"This is exactly the way they act!" Igor said.

"No, please—Master, we aren't making fun of you—honestly!" I said.

"What is this Master, Master crap?" Master Yee asked, brandishing his container of yogurt.

"Teach us, Master!" the Indiana Zephyr shouted, and fell to his knees, his forehead touching the floor. We all did the same thing. "Teach us! Teach us, Master!" We'd seen a couple of kung-fu movies on TV and it was all coming back to us.

"Loonies!" Master Yee shouted. "Loonies! You boys loonies! You get out! Get out now! Crazy people make Yee nervous!"

"Teach us! Teach us!" We remained in position, foreheads touching the floor.

Then Master Yee's voice changed. He spoke softly, lovingly—almost as if he were afraid. "Yes, yes. You nice boys. Yee will teach you. Anything you say. Yee is your friend, right? You go away quiet now. Sometime maybe you come back, do some laundry, okay? Now you all get up, go away quiet. Ladies come soon, do laundry. We not want to scare ladies, okay? You boys go. Try to stay away from take drugs after this, okay? Now you get up, go away quiet, okay, nice boys?"

It was touching to hear the tenderness and concern in the voice of the Zen master. We got to our feet and made a low bow to him.

"That's right—you boys go now. Don't take any more dope, okay, boys? You go home, lie down. Not do any crimes, okay?"

We bowed deeply and left the Balkan Falcon Memorial Laundromat and Shrine of Buddha. We walked in the street in silence for a while, unable to speak after our profound experience.

Finally, the Honorable Venustiano Carranza (President of Mexico) spoke. "What a great man! How fortunate we are! Did you hear all that wisdom? He wants us to be good men—not to

take drugs or do crimes. Isn't that simple, basic moral advice? And he didn't want us to scare the ladies that come into the Laundromat. Wow, are we lucky!"

"So do you think we ought to carve some stuff out of potatoes, or what?" Captain Colossal asked.

"You heard what he said," Igor said. "He wants us to come in and do laundry. It's so simple, yet so perfect."

"Perfect," El Presidente said, "Brother Dharma Ducks, we are on the high road to enlightenment."

IV

We just want the facts, ma'am.

—Sgt. Friday

That night the Dharma Ducks met for the first time to practice the noble meditation of Zen.

We met at the very home of our esteemed leader, the Honorable Venustiano Carranza (President of Mexico). This was a rare honor for the Wild Zen Dada Ducks, because the unenlightened parents of El Presidente had long since made it known that we were not particularly welcome in their house. As avant-garde artists, we were accustomed to this kind of treatment. We did not blame the Honorable Venustiano Carranza for the retrograde attitude of his parents.

On this particular night the parents of the Honorable had gone to a meeting of an organization to which they belonged, the Anti-Communist White Americans League. This was a social organization engaging in good fellowship and harmless fun. With the neanderthal parents of our leader out of the house, the Dharma Ducks were able to meet for serious Zen study.

The Honorable Venustiano Carranza (President of Mexico) turned on the video recorder, taping the two rerun episodes of *Dragnet* which were broadcast back-to-back every night opposite the evening news (this was a service he performed for his parents once a week while they attended their meeting), and as a gesture of affirmation of technology, which we had all learned to love as Dadaists, he set his Apple computer to playing chess against itself, a process which took hours, since the machine never made a mistake.

So, with a machine watching television, and another playing with itself, the Dharma Ducks were relieved of having to carry on these two time-consuming activities, and were free to enter into meditation.

Using pillows from El Presidente's bed, bunched-up raincoats, and whatever else came to hand, the Zen Dada Ducks made meditation seats. We then settled down on the floor of the bedroom of the Honorable Venustiano Carranza (President of Mexico) and attempted to enter into deep meditation.

"How do we know if this is working?" Captain Colossal asked after a few minutes.

"I don't know," El Presidente said. "Just keep at it."

"I feel something," Igor said.

"What? What do you feel?" I asked.

"It's . . . it's like . . . leg cramps," said Igor.

"Look, everybody be quiet for ten minutes, okay?" the Indiana Zephyr said.

After about three minutes Igor asked, "How do we know when ten minutes is up?"

Then the Dharma Ducks watched one of the *Dragnet* reruns and made gray eggs in the microwave oven. Then the parents of the Honorable Venustiano Carranza (President of Mexico) came home and told us that we were homosexual devil worshippers, and that God was going to kill us.

It was a pleasant evening, and all of the Dharma Ducks felt that we'd gotten off to a pretty good start as Zens.

V
Next to Godliness

The following day Igor appeared at Himmler High School with a shaven head. The Dharma Ducks admired the bald knob of Igor, which was hideous and bumpy. After a quick trip to the pharmacy for a razor at the beginning of the lunch period—and another trip for bandages and antiseptic at the end of the lunch period—all of the Wild Zen Dadas had beautiful heads like Igor's.

Shortly after lunch the Dharma Ducks were once again suspended by the Lord High Executioner, also known as the nonexistent Horace Gerstenblut, vice-principal and fascist dictator. We, serious Zens, politely asked the delusionary Gerstenblut why we were being driven out of school. The non-Gerstenblut said that we knew very well why—it was because we had shaved our heads. "Stay away for a whole week!" the executioner had said. "Don't come back until there is visible fuzz."

The behavior of the Lord High Executioner was strange indeed—but such are the ways of the nonexistent. This unlooked-for suspension gave the Dharma Ducks much joy because it meant we could be reunited with our dear Zen master that much sooner. There was, of course, the matter of the notes our parents had to sign—but this was of little consequence— frequent purges, political upheavals, and outbreaks of anti-Dada sentiment had resulted in any number of suspensions. We would have been incompetent Zen Dada Ducks indeed if we had not been able to sign our parents' names.

Less than an hour after our interview with the unsympathetic Gerstenblut, the five Zennists arrived at the Balkan Falcon Memorial Laundromat and Shrine of Buddha with armloads of laundry. We were ready to begin our training under Master Yee.

This was also a chance to perform a service for our families—except in the cases of Igor and the Indiana Zephyr, whose mothers had just done the family wash, and therefore had to bring clean laundry.

Master Yee pretended not to recognize us at first.

"Hello, five bald-headed men," the enlightened one said.

The Dharma Ducks were delighted by this Zen drollery.

Then, Master Yee said, "Oh no! Teenage gang is back! Why you all bald? Drugs make hair fall out! You go away, bald-headed boys! No more hang around! This laundry! Place of business! Go away now! Go drug treatment center! Psychiatric clinic! Go do teenage crimes somewhere else! Go have rumble with other teenage gang! Go crazy, listen to rock 'n' roll! Go stand on corner, frighten people. Leave Yee alone! Go!"

"Master! We have brought laundry!" the Honorable Venustiano Carranza (President of Mexico) said, holding up his bundle of laundry.

Master Yee hesitated, "Okay, do laundry—then go. Not do anything weird, okay?"

In a short time each Dharma Duck was sitting on the floor in front of a washing machine, meditating and watching the wash swirl in the little round window. Master Yee walked up and down, giving us instructions in typical cryptic Zen style. "Why you don't sit in chair?" he asked. "Why you all go bald all a sudden?" He was testing our concentration. We stared resolutely at the swirling wash, thrilled that at last we were receiving the true teaching of Zen.

Naturally, in the presence of our beloved teacher, we made much better progress as meditators. The steady hum and slosh of the washing machines, the cleanliness, the Spartan simplicity of the Balkan Falcon Memorial Laundromat and Shrine of Buddha, and most of all, the muttered prayers and philosophical questions of Master Yee—all combined to make the inward experience more exquisite.

"Where these boys come from?" Master Yee intoned as he walked up and down, inspecting our progress. "Why they all go bald? What kinda drug they take, make them all go bald like that? Why they all sit on floor like that? Some kinda strange boys."

These questions were the famous Zen koan, about which Captain Colossal had read in a Dr. Wizardo comic book. The purpose of these questions is not to be answered as such, but to exercise the mind and deepen the concentration. We were lucky, all right, in having found our teacher.

Finally, during the dryer phase of our meditation, Master Yee addressed us all with a profound question for study.

"Okay, you laundry all finish," our esteemed teacher said, "What you do now?"

"Our laundry all finish," we responded in unison. "What we do now?"

"Our laundry all finish. What we do now?"

"Our laundry all finish. What we do now?"

"Our laundry all finish. What we do now?"

"Our laundry all finish. What we do now?"

It became a chant as we folded the laundry carefully, consciously, mindfully. It was, as we

later agreed, the highest moment yet in our
spiritual and artistic experience.

Always miles ahead of us, the Zen master,
seemingly irrationally, became agitated. "Okay!
Okay! Now you go! You get out! You crazy
boys! You go home now! You crazy bald-head
boys!"

It was precisely the right thing to do. The
master's outburst shook us loose from our moment of detachment and brought us into con-
frontation with reality. This was exactly what
had happened to Dr. Wizardo in Captain Colossal's comic book.

In single file, with slow and solemn dignity,
carrying our laundry on upturned hands, the
Dharma Ducks left Master Yee and ventured
into the street and the gathering dusk.

VI
Sharper Than a Kevin's Tooth

Now I must leave the story of the Dharma Ducks and their thrilling quest for enlightenment and recall the darkest period in the otherwise brilliant history of the former Wild Dada Ducks. It is necessary that the reader be acquainted with events that led to the rise to power of one known as Kevin Shapiro.

In our days as exponents of Dada Art, the Wild Dada Ducks engaged in many innocent diversions. One of these was the creation of a work of literature, an ongoing story known as *Kevin Shapiro, Boy Orphan*. The story of Kevin Shapiro was not unlike those in many of the books for teenage readers in the library of Margaret Himmler High School. It dealt with the life of a wretched kid, whose parents were either hopeless drunks, or drug addicts, or loonies. Kevin himself had any number of problems—life was miserable and impossible, and just when things would seem to be about to get better, they would get worse.

Kevin Shapiro, Boy Orphan was different from the novels published for adolescents in that the story never ended. Instead of winding up with a lecture from some kindly adult about moral responsibility and God, and another chance for Kevin, we would just kill him from time to time. This was, on the whole, more satisfying. We would just bring Kevin back for another chapter of tragedy and degradation, and kill him again when it got boring.

This harmless exercise in Art continued for some time, giving pleasure to the Wild Dada Ducks as we ate our lunches or spent time in the original Balkan Falcon Drug Company (of blessed memory). Then, one fateful day, as our leader then and now, the Honorable Venustiano Carranza (President of Mexico) is wont to say, it came to our knowledge that there was in the school a real kid named Kevin Shapiro.

The Wild Dada Ducks, when this portentous news became known, sought out the real-life Kevin Shapiro, studied him from a distance, and instantly loved him.

It so happened that Kevin Shapiro was, by conventional standards, a graceless nerd—a horrible little fellow with no redeeming qualities of any sort. This made the Wild Dada Ducks love him even more. We decided to notify the world in general and Himmler High School in particular that Kevin Shapiro was indeed a person of greatness. This was to be our ultimate work of Dada-consciousness. In the person of Kevin Shapiro we would bring a powerful Artistic realization to all our fellow students, and make Kevin happy in the process.

By various means, such as distributing printed hand-bills in the toilets, we made the students aware of the exceptional being who was unnoticed in their midst. This work succeeded all too well. In a short time Kevin Shapiro was the hero of all the school. No credit at all was given to the principles of Dada or the Wild Dada Ducks. What was more, Kevin was openly hostile to us and our philosophy.

Somehow we had expected it all to work out differently. We naively believed that we would be appreciated for bringing Kevin to the school's attention. People would respect us. Girls would go out with us. Dada would be elevated to a new status. A golden age would begin.

Instead, Kevin had his friends drench us with soggy Grape-Nuts cereal. This marked the beginning of a period of disillusionment and despair for the Wild Dada Ducks. In fact, only with the realization that mankind was doomed and the discovery of Zen did the Ducks begin to feel that life contained some possibilities.

Even with the detachment of a Dharma Duck, one feels some sadness still in relating this bleak chapter in Duck history—but it must be told, because in the words of an old Dada Duck saying, once again, fate took its cut.

VII
Così Fan Tutte

This is how fate came to take its cut once again in the matter of Kevin Shapiro. It was during an outdoor rehearsal of the Dharma Ducks' musical project. A project which Igor had begun under the Dada regime was the Dada Kazoo Orchestra. This was a five-piece kazoo ensemble made up of the five Wild Dada Ducks. Igor, our concertmaster, played first kazoo. I, Charles the Cat, played second kazoo. The Honorable Venustiano Carranza (President of Mexico) very ably played third kazoo, and the Indiana Zephyr and Captain Colossal played fourth and fifth kazoos respectively.

The orchestra survived into the Zen period,

becoming the Da-da-ka zu orchestra. Since none of the Dharma (formerly Dada) Ducks can read music, it was a laborious process of learning our parts note by note from tape cassettes. Igor, our musical director, generously made up a bootleg cassette for each of us of the one and only piece we almost knew, *Eine Kleine Nachtmusik* by Wolfgang A. Mozart.

Eine Kleine Nachtmusik means one small nacht music—or music to nacht by. Igor explained to us that Mozart loved to nacht—especially late at night. All the Wild Zen Dada Ducks are fond of nachting too—and that helped us feel close to the composer and understand the music. It was easy to imagine the great Mozart having maybe some beer and salami at one in the morning and composing the favorite piece of music of the Ducks.

The Dharma Ducks were engaged in a sidewalk rehearsal when we saw Kevin. We hadn't seen him for some time. Two seasons had passed since our humiliating experience with the soggy Grape-Nuts—and following our realization that all of mankind is doomed, and our subsequent embracing of the doctrine of Zen, we had hardly given little Kevin Shapiro a thought. We were busy Dharma Ducks, working hard toward enlightenment, and, at the moment, giving a brilliant interpretation of the music of Mozart—we had no time to think about the ingratitude and hostility of Kevin Shapiro, who had once been our pride and joy.

We were in full cry—right in the middle of *Eine Kleine*—when he appeared, at the wheel of a bright red car. It was a convertible—a 1962 Studebaker Lark, perfectly restored, and shining all over. Kevin was smiling, displaying that double row of tiny white teeth. He had on sunglasses. Riding in the car with him were the three most agonizingly beautiful girls anyone had ever seen. Jennifer Podgorny, Susan Dachuck, and Lisa Ogronsky—all of them cheerleaders, and between them possessing the six most famous and thought- and talked-about breasts in Himmler High School.

Never did the Dharma Ducks see any of these girls without experiencing a shriveling sensation all over, a stab of pain in the crotch, and a realization of our profound worthlessness as human beings. To see the three of them together was unbearable agony. To see them, as we now saw them, smiling and fawning over Kevin Shapiro, in that indisputably neat red car was bitter beyond all telling.

Our kazoos made a dying sound. As the convertible rolled past us, Kevin gave us the finger, and the girls tittered.

VIII

Psychoanalysis is that spiritual disease of which it claims to be the cure.

—Karl Kraus

Arriving home, each Dharma Duck learned that the Lord High Executioner, Mr. Gerstenblut, had telephoned. He'd thought over our having shaved our heads, had some question as to just how sane we were, and before we were allowed back in school each of us would have to go and see the Board of Education psychiatrist.

The following day, five stubbly-headed

Dharma Ducks sat on the bench outside the office of Dr. Cookie Mendoza, the Board of Education psychiatrist. The Ducks had been scheduled for five appointments in a row, each of which was to last fifteen minutes. Exactly one hour and a quarter later we were all out in the street—none of us having said anything in the waiting room because it had been possible to hear every word that was spoken through the door of Dr. Mendoza's office.

The kid whose appointment preceded the first of the Dharma Ducks had an interesting problem. It appeared that he was in the habit of crawling inside his gym locker, pulling the door shut after him, and making moaning noises, thus frightening the other students. A rumor that the locker room was haunted had gotten started, and many of the students were upset. This, while primitive, showed a certain inventiveness. It might have been worthwhile to turn him on to Zen—but he went to another school. Besides, the Dharma Ducks were intent on the direction the psychiatric interview was taking. It was not going well for the kid, whose name was Richard F. Scott, of 5235 Pearl Street.

Dr. Mendoza wanted to know if he masturbated when he hid in his gym locker. Richard said that he did not. Dr. Mendoza explained that it was all right to tell her things like that. She said that their conversation was entirely confidential, and that nothing he said would go beyond that room. We listened to this with interest. Then she asked him again if he didn't masturbate when he was in the gym locker. Richard repeated that he did no such thing. I believed him.

"Look, Richard, if we are going to help you, you're just going to have to trust me," Dr. Mendoza said. "Now, there's nothing wrong with masturbating. Everybody does it. Now, wouldn't you feel better if you just admitted that the reason you get inside the gym locker is so you can masturbate?"

Richard stuck to his guns. He was starting to cry. He swore that the only reason he got inside his gym locker was to make ghostly noises. Dr. Mendoza said that he was resisting the treatment, and that she'd have to write that in her report to his parents and to the school.

"I thought everything we said in this room was confidential," Richard F. Scott blubbered.

"We're trying to help you, Richard, if you'd only let us," Dr. Mendoza said. Then Richard's fifteen minutes were up. He looked shaken when he came through the waiting room. The Dharma Ducks gave him the thumbs-up sign, but there was no cheering up Richard F. Scott of 5235 Pearl Street. Then it was Igor's turn.

"Well, Maurice, why did you shave your head?" Dr. Mendoza asked.

Maurice is Igor's slave name.

"We all did it," Igor said. "We were just kidding around."

"You know, a great many young people are

getting involved with cults these days," Dr. Mendoza said. "You aren't involved in something like that, are you—you and your friends? You can tell me anything."

"Naw," Igor said.

"Maurice, how do you and your friends spend your time?"

"Uh. Well, it's embarrassing—can I talk about it?"

"Of course. Everything we say in this room stays in this room. You can talk about anything, Maurice."

"Well, we like to buy magazines, uh, with pictures of naked ladies, and uh, then we . . ."

"You masturbate?"

"Uh. Yeh."

"Now, Maurice, I want you to know that is perfectly normal for a boy of your age. There is nothing abnormal about masturbating. You don't have to feel guilty or embarrassed, okay?"

"Okay."

"How many times a day would you say you masturbate, Maurice?"

"Fifteen, maybe twenty times."

"As much as that? Well, you are a healthy and well-adjusted boy, Maurice. And now you know that you don't have to feel guilty about it, right?"

"I thought I did. I thought I had to feel guilty about it."

"No, Maurice, you're just fine—just a fine,

healthy young boy. Don't you worry about anything, okay?"

"Okay."

"And you won't upset Mr. Gerstenblut by doing silly things like shaving your head anymore, will you?"

"No, ma'am."

"And when you get an impulse to do something silly like that, what will you do instead?"

"Masturbate?"

"That's right, Maurice! It's been a pleasure to meet you. Now, please send the next boy in."

Igor was brilliant. It was all we could do not to break into applause.

The interviews of the rest of the Dharma Ducks were more or less identical to Igor's, except that Captain Colossal told Dr. Mendoza that he masturbated thirty times a day. Of course, in his case it was the truth.

IX
The Sorrows of Young Zensters

When we approached the Balkan Falcon Memorial Laundromat and Shrine of Buddha, we saw that Kevin's red car was parked outside. We looked in through the window. Kevin was doing laundry. Jennifer Podgorny, Susan Dachuck, and Lisa Ogronsky were helping him, and smiling and laughing, and touching Kevin a lot. Master Yee was smiling too—and laughing, and beaming at Kevin. Through the open door we heard our Zen master say, "Mr. Shapiro, you nice boy. Do laundry—help your mother. Nice girls with tremendous knockers help you do laundry, yes? Such a nice boy. You mother much be proud, yes?"

"Sure," Kevin said, "I always help my mother. I'm a nice boy, right, girls?"

The girls all laughed as though Kevin had actually said something funny.

"I don't feel like doing my Zen exercises right now," the Indiana Zephyr said. No one else said anything. It would have been bad enough getting caught meditating by Kevin Shapiro, but Jennifer, Susan, and Lisa and their breasts were too intimidating even for the brave Dharma Ducks. We left the Balkan Falcon Memorial Laundromat and Shrine of Buddha and headed for our respective homes.

After our parents had finished yelling at us, abusing us, and threatening us, and after we had had our suppers, we drifted back to the Balkan Falcon Memorial. Kevin was gone of course—but we felt a little strange around Master Yee. Of course we trusted our beloved teacher, and knew that even his seemingly most irrational action was a potential fountain of wisdom, but what could he have had in mind, kissing up to Kevin like that? For his part, the Master mostly ignored us on this occasion. He didn't seem to want to instruct us. For our part, none of us wanted to do our usual meditation.

The Dharma Ducks bought cups of coffee from the machine, and sat in the plastic chairs, nibbling the edges of the plastic foam cups. There was a deep Zen silence in the Balkan Falcon Memorial Laundromat and Shrine of Buddha. A cold breeze blew through the open door.

The lights seemed dim. The coffee grew cold and bitter.

For a time there were failed attempts to begin a conversation. Then the Ducks sat motionless, staring at the coffee congealing in the bottoms of their cups.

Captain Colossal pulled a book out of his jacket pocket. "Tell you what," the Captain said. "I'll read you all a Zen poem, okay?"

If by Rudyard Kipling

If you can keep your head when all about you
  Are losing theirs and blaming it on you,
If you can trust yourself when all men doubt
    you,
  But make allowance for their doubting too;
If you can wait and not be tired by waiting,
  Or being lied about, don't deal in lies,
Or being hated don't give way to hating,
  And yet don't look too good, nor talk too
    wise:

If you can dream—and not make dreams your
    master;
If you can think—and not make thoughts your
    aim;
If you can meet with Triumph and Disaster
  And treat those two imposters just the same;
If you can bear to hear the truth you've spoken
  Twisted by knaves to make a trap for fools,
Or watch the things you gave your life to,
    broken,

*And stoop and build 'em up with worn-out
    tools:*

*If you can make one heap of all your winnings
    And risk it on one turn of pitch-and-toss,
And lose, and start again at your beginnings
    And never breathe a word about your loss;
If you can force your heart and nerve and sinew
    To serve your turn long after they are gone,
And so hold on when there is nothing in you
    Except the Will which says to them: "Hold
    on!"*

*If you can walk with crowds and keep your
    virtue,
    Or walk with Kings—nor lose the common
    touch,
If neither foes nor loving friends can hurt you,
    If all men count with you, but none too much;
If you can fill the unforgiving minute
    With sixty seconds' worth of distance run,
Yours is the Earth and everything that's in it,
    And—which is more—you'll be a man, my
    son!*

Master Yee spoke, "Look, you boys not come
here anymore, see? This final—Yee means it!"

"Not come here anymore? But why, Master?"

"You boys psychologically disturbed," Master Yee said. "Yesterday you all have to go see
Dr. Cookie Mendoza, Board of Education psychiatrist. Yee not want certified loonies hang

130

around laundry, okay? You come back here, Yee call cops—put you all in straitjackets."

"How did you know we went to see Dr. Cookie Mendoza?" the Honorable Venustiano Carranza (President of Mexico) asked.

"Mr. Shapiro tell me," Master Yee said. "Mr. Shapiro good boy."

"How did Kevin Shapiro know we went to see the psychiatrist?" I asked.

"Mr. Shapiro close personal friend of pervert Richard F. Scott, locker room jerk-off artist," the Zen Master said. "Now you go—never come back!"

X

Tzu-mishi-wa and Mishi-gasu

What a blow to the five Dharma Ducks! To be rejected by the Zen Master is the most serious thing that can possibly happen. In one ghastly moment we had been deprived of both our beloved Master Yee and our historic meeting place, the Balkan Falcon. The Zen Dada Ducks were in a state of profound spiritual despair. Moreover, we were standing in the rain.

In one of Captain Colossal's Dr. Wizardo comics there was a story in which the Dr. succumbs to a state of Zen confusion known as tzu-mishi-wa. This comes about because of a psychic spell cast on him by his evil rival, the Pahkman. The danger of being tzu-mishi-wa is that it can lead to mishi-gasu, a state of permanent madness. In the comic book the Dr. has to struggle against his deteriorating state of mind with nothing but his iron will and his autonomic nervous system. The Pahkman almost gets him this time. The Dharma Ducks wondered if we ourselves were not tzu-mishi-wa.

As always, we turned to our leader, the Honorable Venustiano Carranza (President of Mexico) for guidance.

"I say we all kill ourselves," El Presdiente suggested. "We've lost face, and that's a fact. The only way out is honorable ritual suicide."

The idea of making the ultimate gesture of grief was discussed for a while. There were no takers. It was also clear that the Honorable Venustiano Carranza (President of Mexico) was himself hoping to be talked out of the notion.

"You can't kill yourself, Presidente," the Indiana Zephyr said.

"Why not?"

"Well, it will probably hurt. It's likely to be disgusting and messy. The rest of us will be depressed—and when you're all done, you'll be dead."

"Well, then we'll just have to think of something else," our selfless leader said.

"Revenge," I said. "We could take revenge."

"Revenge on whom?" asked Igor.

"Well, it was Kevin Shapiro who told Master Yee that we'd been to the psychiatrist," I said. "We could get Kevin."

"The last time we fooled with Kevin we all wound up with soggy Grape-Nuts stuffed down our pants—remember that," Captain Colossal said. We all remembered that.

"Besides," the Honorable Venustiano Carranza (President of Mexico) said, "it was Yee's intolerant attitude about people who seek psychiatric help that led him to throw us out. Kevin had just told him something that was perfectly true—and nothing to be ashamed of."

"Certainly," the Indiana Zephyr said. "In this day and age there is no stigma attached to having seen a psychiatrist."

"Certainly not."

XI
Furiouser and Furiouser

Horace Gerstenblut, the Lord High Executioner, called the Dharma Ducks to his office.

"I have here the official report from Dr. Cookie Mendoza," the Executioner said. "She says the five of you are vicious little perverts, and utterly preoccupied with unwholesome practices. I could have told her that. Anyway, the doctor has made some very sensible recommendations, which I intend to put into effect. Want to know what they are?"

We nodded.

"Dr. Mendoza suggests that you all be assigned to a disciplinary gym class for three periods each day—that will take the place of your regular gym period and two study periods. She says you need lots of strenuous exercise to take your minds off nasty things. She has also suggested that your gym lockers be taken away, lest you misuse them. And of course a full report will be sent to your parents, with our recommendation that they institute further treatment or punishment as they see fit. I personally hope they skin you alive."

"Mr. Gerstenblut," the Indiana Zephyr said, "you really don't like us, do you?"

"No," said Horace Gerstenblut, "I really don't like you. Now, go straight to the disciplinary gym class—Coach Mohammed is waiting for you."

We walked to the gym. "We are really tzumishi-wa," Igor said.

XII
Zen Christmas

One of the difficulties arising from going to three gym classes every day and not having a locker is that you can't take a shower. We found that out the first time we left our clothes on a bench in the locker room and discovered that other members of the correctional gym class had tied everything into tight knots and had then apparently urinated on the knots. The safest thing was to stay dressed throughout the day. This had the effect of making the Dharma Ducks five very bad-smelling individuals indeed. Our fellow students had never been what you would call close to us—but now they kept the greatest possible distance.

"Look at it this way," Captain Colossal said, "I'll bet none of us catches a cold this semester."

"Plus, we're developing some great muscles doing all those laps and jumping jacks," Igor added.

This conversation took place on the lawn outside the school. The Wild Zen Dada Ducks now endeavored to be out of doors as much as possible—and we had automatically increased our interpersonal distance to about six feet.

The hardest thing for the Ducks was the loss of our Zen Master. It was bleak indeed, having no source of guidance other than back issues of Dr. Wizardo. In addition, our respective parents had inflicted some heavy complications upon us after receiving Dr. Mendoza's report. Captain Colossal was required to see the treacherous Dr. Cookie Mendoza in private sessions. The Indiana Zephyr had to give up his room and sleep in the basement. Igor's parents were negotiating with the parish priest to have their son exorcised. The Honorable Venustiano Carranza was enrolled in the rifle and machine-gun class and Sunday school run by the Anti-Communist White Americans League. I, Charles the Cat, was required to work after school decapitating chickens in the basement of my father's discount poultry market. Winter had set in.

Every now and then we would see Kevin Shapiro in the halls of the school, or driving past in his car. Unless it was actually raining or snowing, the top would be down. The three cheerleaders were always with him. We heard a rumor that Kevin had been accepted for early admission by Princeton University.

At Thanksgiving dinner Captain Colossal's parents announced that they were getting a divorce. They told the Captain it was mostly his fault.

About a week later Igor's dog, Roger, died. Igor had owned Roger for about ten years.

The Indiana Zephyr's hair was not growing back, except for clumps here and there.

The Honorable Venustiano Carranza (President of Mexico) caught pneumonia during a survival exercise with his Sunday school and had to spend a week in the hospital.

I had dreams about the chickens every night.

We were all failing everything except gym.

XIII
Satori Te Salutamus

Even though beset by worldly difficulties, the Dharma Ducks kept up with Zen practice. Having been deprived a second time of our glorious Balkan Falcon, we had to make the best of conditions, and meditate where we could. We experimented with various locations out of doors and the empty garage of the Indiana Zephyr. Finally we settled on my father's place of business, after hours. I had the key. There was a certain coziness to the deserted discount poultry market. Here the Ducks pursued enlightenment, until a certain night.

It was Captain Colossal who spoke first on

that historic evening. "Zen sucks!" the Captain said.

The calm and tranquillity of our inwardness was shattered.

After a long pause Igor said, "It certainly does."

"I've been depressed for months," the Indiana Zephyr said.

I, Charles the Cat, was moved to speak. "I don't think I've ever gotten the hang of this meditation stuff."

"Me, neither," said the Honorable Venustiano Carranza (President of Mexico). "Also, life stinks."

"God, does it ever!"

"And ever since we became Zens, it's stunk worse than usual."

"Right! And why haven't we destroyed Kevin Shapiro?"

"Yeah! How is it we never murdered the little weasel?"

"I want revenge on Dr. Cookie Mendoza!" Captain Colossal shouted.

"And why does Horace Gerstenblut still walk the streets a happy man?"

"Death! Death to Horace Gerstenblut!"

"Our parents are shits!"

"They are! Let's make them suffer!"

The Honorable Venustiano Carranza (President of Mexico) spoke. "Brother Ducks, we have been deluded! We have abandoned Art in favor of religious fanaticism and cheap imported philosophy!"

"But no more!" Igor shouted, waving his copy of *A Boy's Life of Mozart.* "Gentlemen, out with your kazoos! *Eine Kleine Nachtmusik!* Ready? Begin!"

The Dada Boys
in Collitch

[The first chapter of *The Dada Boys in Collitch*, **a novel, to be completed sometime or other.]**

When the Honorable Venustiano Carranza (President of Mexico) went away to college, the loyal Wild Dada Ducks went with him.

I, Charles the Cat, actually applied to and was accepted by Martwist College in upstate New York. The other Wild Dada Ducks, Igor, Captain Colossal, and the Indiana Zephyr, simply packed their suitcases and came with us. Wild Dada Ducks stick together.

Also, the Captain and the Zephyr had not been accepted by any colleges. This was probably because they had filled out all their application forms in tempera paint. Their idea had been to show that they were creative individuals. It was disappointing to know that Harvard, Columbia, and the University of Hawaii had such unenlightened admissions policies.

Igor, in a light moment, had made preliminary inquiries about the Marine Corps—and when the recruiting officer had taken to calling his home and talking to his father, he thought better of the matter, and decided to leave town.

So it was that the Wild Dada Ducks, matriculated and otherwise, set out to seek higher education together—as we had pursued lower education.

It should be noted that the title "Wild Dada Ducks" was something of a holdover from an earlier day during which the Ducks were exclusively Dada artists. This was before we had attained Zen enlightenment and then abandoned Zen forever in favor of dedicating ourselves to the spirit of W. A. Mozart, our ultimate hero. We retained our old nomenclature in the belief that Mozart would have approved of it, had he been able to understand it, Dada regrettably having been as yet undiscovered in Mozart's time.

One of our favorite—if not our very favorite—Dada Duck sayings was, "What would Mozart have done in a case like this?"

The dorm room in Richard M. Nixonn Hall which had been assigned to the Honorable Venustiano Carranza (President of Mexico) and myself was made resplendent by the massed display of Mozart memorabilia belonging to all the Wild Dada Ducks. This consisted of artfully altered rock posters, on which the name and face of Mozart had been added or superimposed in tempera paint by the talented Captain Colossal and the Indiana Zephyr. In addition, there were many pictures and artifacts in the Dada mode honoring Wolfgang. There was a picture of the ham and cheese sandwich (on a bagel) which had been Mozart's favorite, a button (probably) identical to one of Mozart's in a small glass case, Mozart's (facsimile) toothbrush, and an original work by Captain Colossal entitled "Mozart meets Leon Redbone," in which the two culture heros are seated together at the keyboard.

In addition to the two beds, two desks, two chairs, one light fixture, one light bulb provided by the college, as specified in the catalogue, the room also contained the three sleeping bags, suitcases, and various impedimenta of our three brother Ducks. It was a tight fit, and difficult to avoid stepping on outstretched Ducks at night—but the Ducks were together and about to embark on the great educational adventure.

We arrived at Martwist College at night. This was planned in the event that there might be some objection to our moving five people into a room for two. Against the time when a regular way of feeding the extra Ducks would be found, we had provided ourselves with four megasalamis, each over three feet long and sixteen inches in circumference, and a gigantic provolone cheese. These rations could sustain life for weeks in an emergency—and provide healthful midnight snacks for the student Ducks if it developed that other means of nutrition were available.

As it turned out, our preparations were useful, but not strictly necessary. The Martwist College cafeteria did not require identification. They simply fed anyone who turned up. This was probably because the management rightly assumed that anyone not enrolled—that is, anyone who had a choice of eating elsewhere— would automatically do so, self-preservation being the foremost of human instincts. From a Dada perspective, however, the food offered in the college cafeteria was worthy of study. Captain Colossal and Igor both agreed that it was better than what they'd been raised on.

Our other concern, that there might be some objection to the three additional occupants in Room 42, Richard M. Nixonn Hall, ultimately also proved uncalled-for. We were later to learn that in other rooms in the dorm there were to be found still more nonmatriculates, girlfriends, household pets, at least one farmyard animal (a goat), chemical laboratories, and assorted contraband, drugs, firearms, and, it was rumored, a cadaver belonging to a zealous pre-medical student. Richard M. Nixonn Hall was a comfortable place, and the Wild Dada Ducks hoped that for once in our lives we were in congenial and friendly surroundings.

"You know, I really like it here," the Indiana Zephyr said, gnawing on a hunk of salami. Beginning with the first slice taken out of the first mega-salami, our little room was suffused with a homey fragrance which was to make our residence and our persons distinctive for years to come.

"I like it too," Captain Colossal said, "and classes haven't even started yet."

"It is indeed fortuitous that we have come to this fine school," said the Honorable Venustiano Carranza (President of Mexico). "This may be the beginning of the cultural renaissance which we as Dadaists, Zennists, and Mozartians have wished for for so long."

"You guys want to walk around and look the place over?" Igor asked.

The September night was soft and mild as the five Wild Dada Ducks strolled through the campus of Martwist College. The moon illuminated the roofs of the quaint old buildings. Students hurried here and there, greeting one another. The windows of the dormitory rooms shone with a friendly light.

"What a neat place!" the Indiana Zephyr said.

"Hey! Hi, guys!" someone said. The one who had spoken was a youth of six foot two or three

153

inches in height. His hair was brown, and wavy. He had broad shoulders, and a sort of chiseled face, which looked splendid in the moonlight. He stood, hands on hips, feet apart, his long legs terminating in well-worn cowboy boots.

"I am Ronald," the student said. "Ronald Rubin. I am the president of Nixonn Hall."

"That's our dorm!" Captain Colossal said.

"I am also president of the student government, president of the Business Club, the Pre-Law Club, the Investment Club, the Campus Christian Crusade, and captain of the soccer team. I am also related to Leon P. Murtwee, the president of this college. I just want to say, welcome to Martwist College. If there's anything you need—or if you just need to talk things over—feel free to call on me. Also, if you should need to borrow some money, or if you require medical advice—about abortions, for instance, or VD—or investment counseling, just come see me, okay? Also, if you have any complaints—if any of the freshmen seem to be the wrong sort—you know what I mean—just let me know. Any of you guys play any sports?"

"We're all pretty good at croquet," Igor said.

"Yes—well, as I said, if there's anything you need."

We thanked Ronald Rubin. After shaking hands with all of us he left to greet other freshmen.

"What a nice guy," Captain Colossal said.

"He sure is," I said.

The next day the five Wild Dada Ducks attended an inspiring orientation lecture given by a professor whose name we did not catch. It was something like Brontosaurus. Professor Brontosaurus told us how going to Martwist College was the most important thing ever to happen in our lives. He told us that we were going to earn 3.6 times more money for the rest of our lives than we would have earned if we hadn't gone to college. He told us that we were going to be part of the small group of people who would run things in our country. He told us that it was not stuck-up or conceited for us to regard ourselves as better than other people—we *were* better than other people—at least those who hadn't been to college.

The Wild Dada Ducks felt rather important and self-satisfied after listening to Professor Brontosaurus.

"He didn't mention anything about Art or Culture, or Philosophy," Igor said, "or Mozart—I would have expected someone giving a lecture about going to college to have mentioned Mozart."

"All that is taken for granted," the Indiana Zephyr said. "It's assumed that anyone in a college is interested in those things. What the professor talked about was stuff we might never have thought of. For instance, I never knew that I would earn three point six times more money because I'm going to college."

"Technically, you aren't going to college," the

155

Honorable Venustiano Carranza (President of Mexico) said.

"Well, I'm here," the Indiana Zephyr said. "I plan to attend classes. I live in the dorm. I eat in the cafeteria. I'm ready to learn, and discuss ideas, and expand my mind and all that sort of thing. I'd call that going to college."

The next lecture was all about how to register for classes. The matriculated students (in the case of the Wild Dada Ducks, that was El Presidente and myself, Charles the Cat) were given packets of forms to be filled out, and a list of the courses offered and their descriptions. The lecture, given by a lady from the registrar's office, had to do with filling out the forms in ink, and printing carefully. Then we all had to go to the gymnasium and get our forms signed by the professor who would teach each course we had chosen.

First was lunch. This was another fine experience for the Wild Dada Ducks insofar as everything served was Dada food. The most aesthetically advanced dish was Florff, a sort of pink whipped Jell-O dessert. Captain Colossal made up the name for the substance. The Wild Dada Ducks followed the example of the other students and hurled their Florff against the wall of the cafeteria, where the blobs of pinkish stuff made a satisfying noise and stuck among older desiccated blobs thrown in previous semesters.

The Wild Dada Ducks, over cups of inky Martwist College coffee, viewed our fellow students, particularly the female ones. The girls, in turn, looked at us with distaste. This was familiar. The Wild Dada Ducks vowed to find out what changes in our manner and appearance were needed in order to make the Martwist College girls love us—and allow us to love them in return—or at least fondle and bite and slobber on them, as some of the other male students were doing.

The only young woman to return my gaze was Pulkeh Rabinowitz, a very short girl wearing a hand-woven serape with whom I had exchanged a few words at breakfast. I knew her name because she was wearing one of those square cards covered in plastic and printed with the words HI! MY NAME IS PULKEH RABINOWITZ. She appeared to be the only person wearing such a card. Pulkeh Rabinowitz had a guitar slung across her back.

Captain Colossal noticed the direction in which I was looking. "Yes, she is beautiful," the Captain said, echoing my thoughts. "She must be one-fifty if she's an ounce." Captain Colossal tends to judge feminine beauty in terms of pounds on the hoof. He has a subscription to *Opera News*. The Dada Ducks tolerate this perversion. My own appreciation of the glamorous Pulkeh Rabinowitz began with her very thick eyeglasses, an accessory which never fails to turn me on.

"Do you suppose that one such as myself

could win the favor of a girl like that?" I asked half to myself.

"If I don't get her first," Captain Colossal said. "What a fatty!"

I ignored the Captain's vulgarism. What I felt for the beauteous Pulkeh was something mostly spiritual. And, as our leader, the Honorable Venustiano Carranza (President of Mexico) pointed out, this was no time to allow ourselves to be distracted from matters of study. El Presidente and I opened our registration packets, and the Wild Dada Ducks gathered around to choose our courses.

The idea was that the Honorable Venustiano Carranza (President of Mexico) and myself, Charles the Cat, would pick the courses, and our three brother Ducks would sit in if possible, do the reading assignments, and write papers—which would occasionally be handed in under the name of one of the officially registered Ducks. It turned out from our reading of the material in the registration packets that as freshmen we didn't have very many choices. There were a number of courses we were required to take.

College Writing dealt with writing papers, and developing good style, and some fiction and poetry. We all liked this because there would probably be lots of papers, giving all the Dada Ducks a chance to hand in work. Interpersonal Relations, we soon learned, was generally regarded as a "dork" course. It had to do with expressing oneself, and speaking effectively—which made College Speaking, another dorker, even more superfluous than it would have seemed from its title. We thought that we would work up some good topics related to Dada. Freshman Survey was a course that dealt with all of human knowledge in one semester. It was a lecture course, which meant that all the Ducks would be able to attend.

In addition to these required courses, freshmen could also take an optional fifth course. We found a dandy—Mozart, The Man, His Time, His Music and His Eating Habits. A natural for the Mozart-loving Wild Dada Ducks. The Honorable and I hurried off to the gym to get our cards signed.

The Mozart course, it turned out, was canceled because only two students signed up for it. By the time we found this out almost all the other courses were filled, and the only one the Honorable Venustiano Carranza and myself, Charles the Cat, could get into was something called Introduction to Communications. This, as far as we could figure out from the description in the course list, was to deal with things like radio and TV, and newspapers and that sort of thing. It didn't sound too bad, and the professor, Dr. Horst Whistler, was an interesting-looking guy. He wore a tiny snap-brim hat, pointy shoes, blue jeans, a sleeveless yellow T-shirt with a picture of Twisted Sister on it, and one black glove. Sort of sporty.

Having charted our academic course for the semester, the Wild Dada Ducks visited the bookstore. Here the virtue of coming to college as a group was demonstrated again, as each Dada Duck had to pay for only one textbook, thus cutting the individual burden to a fifth. We were impressed to find that the textbooks we were required to buy had in every case been written entirely or in part by the very professor who was teaching the course.

"Wow! These must be some smart guys!" the Indiana Zephyr said.

"These courses are going to be great," Igor said. "I mean, the guy teaching it is the guy who wrote the book."

This distinction tended to offset the fact that the books were quite expensive—between thirty-five and forty-five dollars each—and printed (actually Xeroxed) on cheap paper, and held together in loose-leaf binders.

The Wild Dada Ducks also purchased ballpoint pens, and notebooks with MARTWIST COLLEGE printed on the covers. We then returned to our dorm, where fate had ordained that we should meet the amazing John Holyrood, the Beast of Nixonn Hall.

We found the Beast sitting in our room, munching on an enormous hunk of megasalami. His sandaled feet were resting on a record album on one of the desks, and his rumpled tan raincoat fell loosely about his hips, revealing that he was completely naked underneath.

Noticing the direction of our gaze, the Beast said, "Never fail to permit circulation of fresh air about the testicles—it's exhilarating, and healthful." Then the Beast sprang to his feet, digging his heel into the album, crumpling it slightly, and sending it skittering across the desk. "Gentlemen! Brothers! I was sitting here, pondering, wondering who the occupants of this citadel of taste and culture might be. Actually, I was wondering which of us has the greater mind, Nietzsche or myself. Sometimes I think it's me. Allow me to introduce myself. I am John Holyrood, genius, lover, and philosopher—and you are?"

Sensing that we were in the presence of an extraordinary intellect, we introduced ourselves formally, using our Dada names.

John Holyrood bowed, farted loudly, and gently shook the skirts of his raincoat. "Gentlemen, you are philosophers, and my brothers. I offer you my protection. You will hear things about me. You will hear that I am violent—that I am apt to bite, both in a loving, playful manner, and in earnest, depending on whether you are woman or man. You will hear I am brilliant—that I am importunate, romantic, sentimental, and unsanitary. All of these things are true.

"I am on terminal probation. The dean has his eye on me. One more attempted rape or assault with intent to kill, and I will be suspended but not expelled—and can you guess why? Can you guess why this college does not send me packing? Why Harvard threw me out? Why my parents have gotten an injunction against my coming home? And yet Martwist College tolerates me? Can you guess why?"

John Holyrood was pacing up and down, grinding his teeth and tugging at his beard, which appeared to commence just beneath his eyes. He looked like nothing so much as a movie werewolf about three-quarters through the transformation. We couldn't guess why.

"It is because I am the only really distinguished intellect in this place—except for my mentor, Professor Xavier Wellington, whom I admire and revere about all living men, even though he avoids me. I am the only person here who was ever admitted by Harvard University, not that I have any respect for that elitist shitpile. I am the only genius here—that is, I was, until you came.

"I will guide you, and mold you in my image. You five will also attain greatness. Also I will eat your food, and drink the wine I can't seem to find in any of your luggage, and advise you in matters of philosophy and love."

By this time John Holyrood was squatting on one of the desks, smoking one cigarette after another, and throwing the lighted butts on the floor, on the beds, everywhere. The Ducks picked up the butts and snuffed them in the wastebasket.

"I must tell you of my great love for Pulkeh

Rabinowitz," John Holyrood went on. "Some swine informed her that I had been untrue to her—a great lie. In my heart, at least, I have never wavered. Lust is inconsequential."

It developed that John Holyrood's principal interest in Pulkeh Rabinowitz centered not on her rotundity or her myopia, but on her tiny feet, a feature neither Captain Colossal nor myself had particularly noticed. Holyrood was expounding endlessly on this particular attribute of Pulkeh Rabinowitz when someone passing the open door caught his eye.

With a growl which truly sounded other than human, John Holyrood flew across the room and out the door. We then heard an impact, a scuffling sound, and a scream of anguish. We rushed into the corridor and found Holyrood all over a boy more than twice his size. Dragging the Beast of Nixonn Hall off the unfortunate took the best efforts of the five of us.

"A trifle," the Beast said. "This lout once insulted me in some way or other—at least I think it was he. I'm quite all right. Please don't worry about me." With that, John Holyrood, our first friend at college, the Beast of Nixonn Hall, sauntered down the corridor and out of the building, whistling a tune from *Don Giovanni*.

The Beast's victim, one Ned Calgary, rolled around moaning for a while, and then was helped to his room by a couple of friends. Meanwhile, Ronald Rubin, our dorm president, appeared. He draped his arms over the shoulders of the Wild Dada Ducks, and said, "If I were you, fellows, I wouldn't have anything to do with Holyrood—it will hurt your chances to be popular with the other students." Associating with John Holyrood, the Beast of Nixonn Hall, as well as the flamboyantly homosexual Dick Lupin, the unbelievably smelly Eric Levine, the obnoxious Kent Sweeney (who always wore a suit and tie), and the four-hundred-fifty-pound Bootsie MacIntosh had no effect one way or the other on the social status of the Wild Dada Ducks.

The majority of the students at Martwist College tended to ignore the Wild Dada Ducks. We sensed no hostility—we just felt invisible. For our part, we found it difficult to understand what the other students were all about. Their jokes and greetings and raucous slogans seemed to go right over our heads. Gradually, at mealtimes, we found ourselves sitting with the other freaks. Ronald Rubin ceased to caution us.

It should be stated that the Wild Dada Ducks neither sought the company of these outcasts, nor did we object to them. They were quite simply the only people who were willing to associate with us.

In truth, there were times when we might have objected to John Holyrood, but since he was in the habit of forcing the lock and bursting into the room at any hour of the day or night, and since he also was in the habit of standing outside the door for long periods listening, the Dada Ducks automatically refrained from expressing any negative comments about him. To give John Holyrood offense was a straight road to the infirmary.

Had we expressed our reservations about John Holyrood, they would have dealt exclusively with his social deportment, his personal habits, and his violence. We all respected his intellect.

Another observation the Wild Dada Ducks made during the first couple of weeks of the semester was that our courses were not as stimulating as we had hoped. We anticipated that things might get better in the second semester, or the second year, but for the moment there wasn't a great difference between Martwist College and the four horrible years we had spent at Himmler High.

Encouraged by John Holyrood, the Wild Dada Ducks began to engage in wine drinking. It would be more accurate to say that we engaged in wine purchasing. We seldom got to taste more than a drop before John Holyrood, who appeared to have some kind of sixth sense in these matters, would appear with his private mug, which hung around his neck on a leather thong. We continued to acquire wine because it pleased him, and because he tended to become antisocial when no wine was offered.

I also bravely courted Pulkeh Rabinowitz. This was triply brave because of my inexperience with women, Pulkeh's expressed desire to

experience carnal love (which I shared, but first
wanted to get my hands on a good book on the
subject), and, of course, the matter of John Holyrood's affection for Pulkeh. In the first weeks
of the semester I got as far as having some conversations with Pulkeh always in the presence
of another Dada Duck, or one of Pulkeh's circle
of friends, which was more or less the female
counterpart of ours. In these conversations,
which were general and polite on my part, Pulkeh would usually make some reference to being a junior in college and still never having
experienced pleasure. "Someone is going to
make his move one of these days and receive
the riches of my body," Pulkeh Rabinowitz
would say. Her other interest was folk music.

One night, when all the Wild Dada Ducks
were sleeping, John Holyrood kicked open the
door of our room. He sat on my legs, flicking
hot cigarette ashes on the sleeping bag of the
Indiana Zephyr. He spoke for a while of Nietzsche, as usual, and then said, "Charles, old
pussycat, I know the secret of your heart. I've
seen you with her."

I braced myself for the wild swarming attack
I knew was coming. I could practically feel John
Holyrood's little white teeth. "I just want to
warn you, old fellow," John Holyrood said.
"She's a temptress. She's a succubus. She's a
vampire. She just wants men at her feet. But,
you have my blessing. Take her, Charles, she is

yours—I only ask that you steal one of her tiny sneakers for me."

Then John Holyrood lurched forward, and appeared to be sobbing—but he was throwing up in the wastebasket, as he seemed to do exclusively in our room. "Never mind me," John Holyrood said between eruptions, "I'll be fine."

John Holyrood's nocturnal visit left me with mixed feelings.

Igor had taken to going for long, solitary walks in the woods and fields which surrounded the college. The Wild Dada Ducks, respecting his need for privacy, did not offer to go with him. We assumed he was depressed, or homesick, or disgusted, or crazy—or perhaps just needed to be alone to do those things which are difficult to do when you sleep five in a room. In truth, none of us thought anything of his ambulatory proclivities.

One morning, a Saturday on which there were no classes, Igor addressed his brother Ducks. "You all have to come with me."

"Come with you where?"

"Come walking with me."

"It looks like rain, and we have to study."

"You have to come with me."

"Why?"

"Because there's something I want you to see. Actually, I want to see if you see it."

"What is it?"

"I don't want to say. I don't want to prepare any of you. If you know what you're going to see, and you say you saw it, I won't know if you really saw it or if you're humoring me, or maybe responding to mass-suggestion."

There was a chapter about mass-suggestion in our communications textbook. It seems that large groups of people can imagine amazing and impossible things simultaneously. The book said that once the entire country believed for eight years that Ronald Reagan had been elected president.

"You saw something on one of your walks?"

"On all of my walks."

"And you want to see if we see it?"

"Right. Coming?"

We pulled on our jackets and left the dorm with Igor. He led us across the fields and into the woods that bordered the college. We soon picked up a little path through the woods. It was nice in the woods. I wondered why I hadn't come out here myself. I could ask Pulkeh Rabinowitz, I thought. I was imagining myself ripping her guitar off her on a pile of dry leaves, when we saw the little old man.

"You see anything?" Igor asked.

"The little old man?"

"What's he wearing?"

"A brown corduroy jacket, a sort of golfer's cap, sneakers, eyeglasses."

"That's him!" Igor said, excited.

"Ja, gentlemen, and vhat may I do for you zis morning?" the little old man asked.

"He's always here," Igor whispered.

"What do you mean, always here?" I asked.

"I mean he's always here, no matter what time I come. He's always hanging around in these woods."

"So? Maybe he likes it here."

"No, it's something else. There's something strange about him."

"Maybe he escaped from the looney bin up the road—but he doesn't seem dangerous."

"He's no looney," Igor said. "I think he's supernormal."

While we were standing around discussing him, the little old man looked on pleasantly and smoked a cigarette out of an amber holder, which he held as if it were a pencil, the burning end of the cigarette pointed at the sky.

"Who are you?" the Honorable Venustiano Carranza asked the old man.

"I am Heinrich Bleucher," the old man said. "Ich bin—zhat is, I am—a leprechaun. *Alzo!* Please come viss me now, and vee commence vit zuh pot of goldt."

The old man had a pretty obvious German accent for a leprechaun. He was evidently pretending to be a leprechaun. Or he was pretending to have a German accent. It came and went. Or he was crazy and escaped from the looney bin—but he didn't seem crazy.

"Ja, it iss not zuh sort of pot of goldt you can spend at K Mart," Heinrich Bleucher said. "You cannot buy a Sony Vahlkmahn viss ziss goldt. Ziss goldt goes between zuh ears. Come!"

We followed Heinrich Bleucher through the woods, and soon came to a Ping-Pong table surrounded by eight or nine mismatched kitchen chairs and a couple of wooden crates set on end.

"So, gentlemen, please sit and vee start."

We took chairs around the table.

"Goot! Now, you must all know zhat in prehistoric times man vass evolving from apelike creaturess—ja? You all know ziss?"

We all knew that.

"Ja, zo after a vhile, zhese creaturess vere pretty vell advanced, und could valk around erect, und grunt at vun anozher, und already zhey could paint magnificent picturess on zuh valls of caves, see?"

Heinrich Bleucher held up a book with color pictures of cave paintings. I had seen some of this stuff in an old copy of *Life* magazine once.

"Zhese paintings are zuh goods!" Heinrich Bleucher said. "Not so much painting in zuh zhousands und zhousands of yearss to follow vass better zhan some of ziss stuff. I know about painting—you can take my vord for it. So, zuh guy who painted ziss vass a smart guy, okay? If you try to paint a buffalo like ziss, you vill see it's not so easy to get it right. Ziss painter, vhatever his reasons for making zuh painting—vee come to zhat soon—*he vass no dummy*!

"Zo, should vee say zhat ziss painting is great art?" Heinrich Bleucher took a long drag on his cigarette. "No! It iss not art. Vell, it is art to us, because zhat is how vee look at it—but to

170

zuh caveman who painted it, zuh intention vass not to make an artistic performance. Maybe no-vun vould ever see ziss painting! Zo, you know vhy ziss cave guy painted it in zuh first place? You—young man, vhat iss your name?'

"Charles the Cat," I said, giving my Dada name without thinking.

"Ja, goodt! Ziss is a goodt name. It iss like zuh Dadaists—vee vill talk about zhem also. So, Charles zuh Cat, vhy vass zhis cave bozo paint-ing zuh beautiful painting of zuh caribou, hah?"

It so happened I had just remembered some-thing from the article in the old *Life* magazine. "He probably painted it as part of some rit-ual—something to do with hunting that ani-mal."

"Ja! Bravo! Excellent! Ziss is exactly right! It vass part of a magical performance, so he vould first paint zuh animal, *to catch its soul*, ja, its essence und zhen he hoped zuh tribe vould be able to catch zuh physical animal. Ziss is inter-esting, ja? But more interesting is zhat ziss cave clown vass already trying to *think*. If you con-sider vhat vass known to zhese poor slobs, it isn't such a bad idea—given vhat zhey had to vork vith. So ziss guy is part of a process by vhich man iss already trying to figure out his environment. Nice going, ja?"

It *was* nice going. I felt good about the cave painter. I was really proud of him—and I was really proud of myself for giving a good an-swer. This was the most interesting thing I'd ever gotten into. Looking around, I could see that the other Wild Dada Ducks felt the same way. Igor had brought a notebook, and was writing in it. Evidently he'd had some conversations with Heinrich Bleucher already.

Bleucher continued. "If you like, you can read some anthropoligists about shamanism among zuh Eskimos und zhat sort of zhing, und get a better idea of vhat ziss cave painter vass thinking about. So! Now vee jump a few generations. Vee have modern man, anthropologically speaking, und he isn't writing yet, but he's still trying to figure out his environment. Like zuh cave painter, he still iss observing nature, und he believes there is a soul or essence in zuh things he observes.

"Now you may write ziss down, Mr. Igor, ziss vordt: *Mythopoeia*. You recognize vhat vordts ziss iss made from? You, young man, vhat iss your name?" Heinrich Bleucher pointed to the Indiana Zephyr.

The Indiana Zephyr expressed the opinion that the word sounded like myth and poetry.

"Ja! Brilliant! It is *mythos* und *poiein* in Greek, und zuh vordt hass to do vith zuh making of myths—und now vee are talking about zuh first stage in human thought. Zhese guys in zuh mythopoeic period are valking around thinking zhat zhere are souls, spirits, essences in zuh rocks and trees, ja? Zhey think zuh thunder is zuh farting of zuh gods, und so forth. Ziss covers zuh Greek and Roman gods, all zuh primitive religions, ja? Ziss kind of thinking goes on even today, ja? Modern Hinduism iss still a mythopoeic system—und people who believe in astrology are still vorking in a system of myth, zuh exact same myths zuh ancient Greeks believed in. Okay, so vhat? You, Mr. Igor, so vhat?"

"I don't know so vhat—I mean, so what," Igor said.

"No, of course you do not know so vhat. Zhat is vhat I am going to tell you. Ziss is so vhat—in a system of thought vhich is based on myth, zhere is no free vill! Zhat is so vhat, und it is a big so vhat. If everything zhat can happen to you is already ordained in zuh heavens, or in zuh guts of a chicken—zhey used to cast fortunes vith zuh guts of a chicken, you knew zhat?—zhen you do not decide your own fate. It is decided for you. So, for a long time, mankind had no vay to think about zhings except in ziss mythopoeic framevork. Ziss doesn't mean zhey vere all dummies! Zhat cave painter vass already hot stuff! Und, vhen you look at zuh Hindu sculptures—und some of zhem are *really* hot stuff—und zuh art of Sumeria, und zuh *Iliad* und zuh *Odyssey*, und zuh Greek dramas, zhat is classy, ja?

"But even more classy iss vhen vee come to Socrates, und Buddha, und Jesus, und some other guys—but now it iss time for you to go. Zhank you, gentlemen."

Heinrich Bleucher lit another cigarette. It was clear that he had finished. We wanted more.

"Uh, Mr. Bleucher," Captain Colossal said.

"Ja?"

"Exactly who are you?"

"I told you. I am a leprechaun."

"Excuse me. I don't believe that."

"Oh? You are calling me a liar? Vhy don't you believe zhat I am a leprechaun?"

"Because I am not a mythopoeic guy," Captain Colossal said.

"Goodt! Hot stuff!" Heinrich Bleucher said. "Now you vill all go. Before you come back, maybe you vould like to read zuh *Bhagavad-Gita*. Look in zuh Martwist College library—but zhey probably von't have it, in vhich case, you can buy it off zuh magazine rack in zuh drugstore. Goodt-bye."

We made our way out of the woods, speculating about Heinrich Bleucher.

"Who do you suppose he is?" I asked.

"He's obviously some sort of teacher," the Honorable Venustiano Carranza (President of Mexico) said, "but he's nothing like the professors at Martwist College."

"And you say he's been here every time you come out to the woods?" we asked Igor.

"Every single time," Igor said. "The first time I met him, I just assumed he was this old guy taking a walk, like I was doing. That time he talked about Confucius and Lao Tze."

"Who or what are they?"

"Neat guys. Sometime you should try to get him to talk about them."

"So then what happened?"

"So we had a nice time. Bleucher talked about Confucius and Lao Tze, and I sort of followed most of what he was talking about; and that was all. Then I met him again, and this time he talked about Einstein and the history of modern physics, and quantum mechanics, and Niels Bohr and Max Planck, and those guys. Then another time he told me all about life in ancient Greece. By the way, so far I haven't been able to find one single book he talked about in the college library. Anyway, I started to get a spooky feeling about Heinrich Bleucher. I mean, why is he in the woods all the time? And why couldn't I find any of the books he talked about? Well, I started to wonder if I wasn't imagining him. That's why I wanted you guys to come with me."

"That's some reason," the Indiana Zephyr said. "Otherwise I suppose you would have just kept him to yourself, huh? I'm really pissed that I missed the talk about physics."

"You've got to understand—I wasn't sure I wasn't hallucinating. He always wears those exact same clothes, and he never gets dirty or anything—and I don't think he ever goes anywhere. Do you think he's a ghost, maybe?"

"If ghosts smoke Camels, he might be," Captain Colossal said. "I think he's a retired professor, and he's got no place to go, so he hangs around in the woods—probably he likes nature. When you came along, he just started talking about stuff he's interested in. At any rate, I for one am going back tomorrow."

"I don't see what strikes you as so supernatural," the Honorable Venustiano Carranza (President of Mexico) said. "You didn't see him dematerialize or levitate or anything neat like that, did you?"

We all laughed at that point. I thought Igor was going to say something, but when we laughed, he just looked frustrated and said nothing.

By this time we had gotten back to our room. Upon opening the door, we were confronted with a spectacle of unbelievable destruction and horror. Papers were strewn everywhere, our costly textbooks were crumpled and sloshed with red wine. Smoldering cigarettes made little black nimbuses on the carpet. What had apparently been a vigorous wastebasket fire was still flickering weakly, and a pall of smoke hung beneath the ceiling.

Most horrible was the damage wrought on our Mozartiana collection—no, that was second or third most horrible. Most horrible, for certain, was the ghastly fragrance of unwashed bodies having recently engaged in strenuous and exciting activity. And horrible was the spectacle of *two* sets of pudgy white thighs protruding from rumpled tan raincoats side by side on the beds, which had been shoved together and covered with the sleeping bags of the three ancillary Ducks. Right calves balanced comfortably on left knees, toes wiggling, feet bobbing in unison; it seemed for a moment that John Holyrood had somehow cloned—but it was stunningly evident that one naked nether half was male and the other female.

What had happened was all too clear—John Holyrood, who had shown signs of being in rut for the past few days, had mated—and he had done it in our room!

"Oh Jesus God!" Captain Colossal said.

Amid the debris there were a few dainty objects of feminine attire. A guitar with two broken strings lay in the corner. A pair of thick-lensed eyeglasses lay carelessly tossed on a desk.

"Hi!" Pulkeh Rabinowitz said shyly. "I came up here looking for you"—speaking to me—"and John came in and said he was depressed. He let me comfort him. It was beautiful. John has such a sensitive nature."

There was hardly anything in the room left undestroyed. The worldly possessions of the Wild Dada Ducks, as well as my hopes of being the Edmund Hillary to Pulkeh Rabinowitz's Mount Everest, had been immolated in John Holyrood's (it couldn't have been more than) two hours of love.

"I'm feeling much better," John Holyrood said. "Please don't worry about me."

Their arms around each other, wearing noth-

177

ing but their raincoats, the lovers left the room, gazing fondly, eye to eye.

"Holy shit!" said the Indiana Zephyr.

"What do we do, burn all this stuff?" Igor asked.

"I'm not touching anything without gloves," Captain Colossal said.

"We're wiped out," I said.

"Destroyed," said the Honorable Venustiano Carranza (President of Mexico).

Ronald Rubin appeared. "So you finally decided to unlock your door," he said. He handed us a piece of paper. "This is a summons, from the Campus Christian Crusade and the Student Court—which have recently been consolidated into one body. You are to appear at eight tonight to face charges of moral turpitude, setting a fire, and conducting an orgy. If you don't show, we're going to whip your asses something terrible."

"Evidently, they heard Holyrood in here," I said.

"I can imagine that," said Igor. "It must have sounded like the five of us at least."

"Well, we'll explain all this to the Student Court," I said. "After all, we've got truth on our side."

"And they've got God on their side," Captain Colossal said. "They're going to destroy us."

"But even if we'd done all this," I said, "it isn't so different from things everybody here does. Ronald Rubin is balling that creepy little girlfriend of his constantly—and those guys on the third floor have weird parties all night long. And as to destruction of property, this whole building looks bombed—the only difference is that now our room looks like most of the others. What can they do to us?"

Ronald Rubin poked his head into the room. "Oh, by the way, the Christian Crusade/Student Court has the power to impose punishments, levy fines, and we can also advise the administration to suspend or expel you, or turn you over to the civil authorities—and, just between ourselves, seeing that you haven't got any friends, there's no reason we shouldn't grind you into shit. And I heard what you said about Nancy, who is a virtuous Christian girl—and guess who's president of the court."

"You?"

"No, Nancy. She hates your guts. See you tonight, freaks."

"No chance," Igor said.

"None," said the Indiana Zephyr.

"What would Mozart have done in a case like this?" asked the Honorable Venustiano Carranza (President of Mexico).

It was so easy! Five minutes later we were in John Holyrood's room. The smitten Pulkeh Rabinowitz had been sent out by her new lover to find instant whipped cream to use in some innovative way. We had heard his instructions, and her tiny sandals clicking down the stairs. John Holyrood was alone. We kicked open the door and rushed him. It was undoubtedly because of his recent expenditure of energy, but immobilizing John Holyrood was no problem for the five furious Ducks. In seconds, ten bony knees pressed relentlessly down on various parts of John Holyrood's body.

"Now, gentlemen," Holyrood wheezed, "there's no call to become irate. Remember what a good friend I've been to you."

"You're a shit, Holyrood," I hissed, thumping his head rhythmically on the floor. None of us had ever seen the inside of John Holyrood's room. It was tidy! It had a color television, a sheepskin rug, a little wooden cart with bottles of wine and liquor! There was a coffee table with a little glass bowl full of jelly beans. Copies of *Playboy* neatly overlapped on the table. There was nothing in the way of desk or books or anything in the room to suggest that the inhabitant was a student—or a well-known slob, iconoclast, and beast.

The Honorable Venustiano Carranza (President of Mexico) increased the pressure of his knee on Holyrood's windpipe. "Just tell me this, shitball," El Presidente said, "have you ever actually read anything by Nietzsche?"

"My cousin has," gasped the asphyxiating Holyrood, "he went to Harvard, no fooling!"

"To business," said Igor. "You ruined our stuff, you creepy scum. Pay for it!"

"Honestly, I haven't got any money," Holyrood rasped.

"Kill him," I said.

The Dada Ducks shifted their weight, kneeling a little more heavily on the Beast of Nixonn Hall.

"It's in the top drawer!" the agonized Beast wailed.

Captain Colossal opened the drawer and produced a fat wad of bills. He counted. "Three hundred and forty-five dollars. Think that will cover the damage?"

"Barely," said the Indiana Zephyr, who was busy hacking away at John Holyrood's beard with his Swiss Army knife, "but we'll take it. Any objections, turd?"

"Lay off my beard!" the Beast begged—but too late—he was half-shorn.

"Any objection to our taking this money to pay for all the stuff you defiled?" the Zephyr asked, eyeing Holyrood's member, in evidence as usual. "I've seen entirely too much of that thing," he added.

"Take the money!" Holyrood shrieked. "It's only fair. I'm sorry I messed up your stuff."

"Right," said the Wild Dada Ducks, who then tied the Beast of Nixonn Hall hand and foot, gagged him, and stuffed him into his closet.

"We'd better get completely out of here," I suggested.

"True," the Indiana Zephyr said. "We're outlaws now."

"When Pulkeh comes back and finds Holyrood, he'll probably say we came in here and robbed him."

"Who'd believe that? It was only because he was postcoital that the five of us were able to overpower him."

"The shits who run everything in this place would believe him because he'd be telling them incriminating stuff about us, and we're scheduled to be lynched as it is."

"Let's buy some time," Captain Colossal said. He opened the door of the closet. "Hey, Beast, I'm writing a letter to your girlfriend. I'm going to say that you were just using her mediocre body, and that you've had better sex with the family Basset hound at home—and that anyway your real lover is Ronald Rubin. Now I'm signing your name—and let's add a P.S. Oh, yes, folk music sucks! Okay, Beast?" John Holyrood growled and strained at the tape on his wrists and ankles.

"Don't antagonize him," Igor said. "He's going to work himself loose as it is."

"It'll take hours," the Captain said. "I'll tape this note to the door of his room. Pulkeh won't forgive him until after supper at the earliest."

"By which time we'd better be gone," I said.

"Agreed," said the Indiana Zephyr. "Where shall we go, home?"

"Not home!" I said. "That was the only good thing about this shitball college—it's not home. I say let's take to the woods, and hang out with Heinrich Bleucher."

"He's supernatural," Igor said.

"He's smart, and he can teach us stuff," I said. "We've heard your supernatural theory."

"There are things I didn't tell you," Igor said.

"Tell us later," the Honorable Venustiano Carranza (President of Mexico) said. "We've just got a little time to see what we can salvage from our room—and then we need to stop at the army-navy store and buy a tent and some other equipment. And then, let's stop off at the drug-store and see if they really have a copy of the *Bhagavad-Gita*."

THE DRAGON REBORN

Sequel to *The Great Hunt*

Book Three
~ of ~
The Wheel of Time

by

Robert Jordan

Praise for *Eye of the World*

"A powerful vision of good and evil...fascinating people moving through a rich and interesting world." —Orson Scott Card

"Richly detailed...fully realized, complex adventure."
—*Library Journal*

"A combination of Robin Hood and Stephen King that is hard to resist...Jordan makes the reader care about these characters as though they were old friends." —*Milwaukee Sentinel*

Praise for *The Great Hunt*

"Jordan can spin as rich a world and as event-filled a tale as [Tolkien]...will not be easy to put down." —*ALA Booklist*

"Worth re-reading a time or two." —*Locus*

"This is good stuff...Splendidly characterized and cleverly plotted...The Great Hunt is a good book which will always be a good book. I shall certainly [line up] for the third volume."
—*Interzone*

The Dragon Reborn
coming in hardcover in August, 1991

BESTSELLERS
FROM TOR

☐ ☐	50570-0	**ALL ABOUT WOMEN** *Andrew M. Greeley*	$4.95 Canada $5.95
☐ ☐	58341-8 58342-6	**ANGEL FIRE** *Andrew M. Greeley*	$4.95 Canada $5.95
☐ ☐	52725-9 52726-7	**BLACK WIND** *F. Paul Wilson*	$4.95 Canada $5.95
☐ ☐	51392-4	**LONG RIDE HOME** *W. Michael Gear*	$4.95 Canada $5.95
☐ ☐	50350-3	**OKTOBER** *Stephen Gallagher*	$4.95 Canada $5.95
☐ ☐	50857-2	**THE RANSOM OF BLACK STEALTH One** *Dean Ing*	$5.95 Canada $6.95
☐ ☐	50088-1	**SAND IN THE WIND** *Kathleen O'Neal Gear*	$4.50 Canada $5.50
☐ ☐	51878-0	**SANDMAN** *Linda Crockett*	$4.95 Canada $5.95
☐ ☐	50214-0 50215-9	**THE SCHOLARS OF NIGHT** *John M. Ford*	$4.95 Canada $5.95
☐ ☐	51826-8	**TENDER PREY** *Julia Grice*	$4.95 Canada $5.95
☐ ☐	52188-4	**TIME AND CHANCE** *Alan Brennert*	$4.95 Canada $5.95

Buy them at your local bookstore or use this handy coupon:
Clip and mail this page with your order.

Publishers Book and Audio Mailing Service
P.O. Box 120159, Staten Island, NY 10312-0004

Please send me the book(s) I have checked above. I am enclosing $ _____
(please add $1.25 for the first book, and $.25 for each additional book to cover postage and handling.
Send check or money order only—no CODs).

Name _____
Address _____
City _____ State/Zip _____
Please allow six weeks for delivery. Prices subject to change without notice.

THE BEST IN
SCIENCE FICTION